"To us, Di," he said softly. His smile was enigmatic.

"Which 'us' is that, Harrup? You and I and Lady Selena? Or is it you and I and Mrs. Witby? Perhaps all four of us? I have heard of romantic triangles, but if you actually think to involve me in a—a rectangle, I must tell you—"

"I have no interest in polygons. A straight line is what I shall be walking in the future. A straight line, the shortest distance between two points. First I mean to eliminate the distance between us."

Harrup put his glass aside and drew Diana up from her seat into his arms. She was crushed to his chest while his lips pressed ruthlessly on hers. Nothing had prepared her for the sweep of emotions that surged over her, making her want to cry and laugh, dance and shout and sing all at once. His lips moved hungrily on her, and she answered every deman around his nec

Fawcett Books
by Joan Smith:

BABE

BATH BELLES

THE BLUE DIAMOND

A COUNTRY WOOING

THE DEVIOUS DUCHESS

LACE FOR MILADY

LADY MADELINE'S FOLLY

LETTERS TO A LADY

LOVE BADE ME WELCOME

LOVE'S HARBINGER

LOVER'S VOWS

RELUCTANT BRIDE

REPRISE

ROYAL REVELS

STRANGE CAPERS

TRUE LADY

VALERIE

WILES OF A STRANGER

LETTERS TO A LADY

Joan Smith

FAWCETT CREST • NEW YORK

A Fawcett Crest Book
Published by Ballantine Books
Copyright © 1987 by Joan Smith

Library of Congress Catalog Card Number: 87-91535

ISBN 0-449-21161-4

Manufactured in the United States of America

First Edition: October 1987

Chapter One

"You must not worry your head about Ronald's finding a position, my dear." Miss Peabody smiled fondly. "Chuggie will be only too happy to find him something with the government. Always so kind and thoughtful. You have only to say the word and Chuggie will do it. He is the most obliging creature in nature, and so well placed, too, in the cabinet."

Diana Beecham regarded her chaperon with a leery eye and smiled a noncommittal smile, wondering how a lady who looked so sane could be so foolish. Miss Peabody had a long, lean body and a long, thin face—the kind of face that looked intelligent and was frequently compared to a hatchet. Her eyes, too, were sharp and fast, but in the matter of Lord Harrup they were purblind.

Miss Peabody held strong and unique views regarding this selfish gentleman's obligingness. The reason for this, as for the dame's calling a thirty-five-year-old marquess and privy councillor "Chuggie," was old and well known to her listener. Miss Peabody, Harrup's distant cousin, had been his nanny. Having no babe of her own on whom to spend her maternal instincts and aspirations, she had lavished them with fine indiscrimination on her charge. Many a dull evening had Diana been regaled with Lord Harrup's nursery antics: walking at nine months, talking a blue streak at fifteen, reading at three years. It was really astonishing it had taken his lordship the usual number of years to graduate from university, when you stopped to think about it. That this mental marvel got no better than a gentleman's "C" was equally surprising. The professors, Miss Peabody had assured her, had all been jealous as green cows of Chuggie's genius.

Diana feared the tales of Harrup's obligingness were equally exaggerated. To her knowledge, all he had ever done for Miss Peabody was to pass her on to his neighbors, the Beechams, when he had no further use for her. There she had held sway over the Beecham nursery, later graduating to governess and finally to chaperon when Mrs. Beecham passed away. Whether a young lady now in her twenty-fifth year required any other guide and protector than her father was a moot point. Diana considered Peabody a companion and friend. It was true Harrup called on Miss Peabody several times a year, often stuffing a fat envelope into her fingers. It was scanty enough reward from a gentleman who had ten thousand a year at his disposal, and lived in palatial luxury himself. But it was those envelopes, Diana thought, that *really* accounted for the high esteem in which he was held.

Whether he would be eager to find a position at Whitehall for Diana's brother Ronald, just graduated from Oxford and wanting to get started in a political career, was another matter. As Lord Harrup was their most influential neighbor and friend, however, the matter would certainly be presented for his consideration.

"I told Ronald to call on him. I thought we would have heard by now," Diana said, and rose to stroll restlessly about the blue saloon. The chamber, like the house, was comfortable and pretty without claiming much grandeur. Sun shone through the trees of the park, making patterns on the lawn. It was a fine day in late April—a shame to waste such a day indoors, when her mare would be champing for exercise. But Miss Peabody had ordered the dolly out, which meant Diana had to make frequent trips belowstairs to see the laundry was not being overbleached.

Unlike Lord Harrup, the majority of the world was in a conspiracy to plague Miss Peabody and thwart her every wish. The very weather itself had it in for her. Winds sought out her sensitive ears and caused them to ache with monotonous regularity. Servants purposely broke her favorite dishes. Indeed, any dish that hit the floor immediately became a favorite. Cook, knowing she liked her beef rare, burned it to cinders, and the laundress would certainly destroy her blue muslin with bleach if Diana were not there to monitor the application. Diana was another of the blessed ones. She and Ronald rated just a few notches below Harrup in the dame's esteem.

"Oh, there is the postman!" Diana exclaimed, and hastened to the door. "There should be a letter from Ronald."

The expected letter did not arrive. The new issue of *La Belle Assemblée* was there, the cover in shreds by the ill offices of the postman, but of greater interest was a letter franked by Lord Harrup and addressed to Miss Peabody, who blushed like a schoolgirl when Diana handed it to her.

"Dear me, what can Harrup have to say?" she exclaimed, and grabbed the envelope. Harrup was only Chuggie when she was extolling his virtue. She read the letter swiftly and said, "It is really to both of us. He writes, 'Dearest Peabody'—he always calls me dearest—'Would you or Di be kind enough to send a footman to Hitchin to pick up some documents for me? They are with a Mrs. Whitby (map enclosed). I had hoped to pick them up myself en route to London yesterday, but Mrs. Whitby was not at home. I left a note requesting her to have them ready. They are too sensitive to entrust to the mail. Please take them to Harrup Hall. The next carriage coming to London can bring them to me. I thank you in advance, knowing you will not fail me. Sincerely, Harrup.' " She smiled dotingly at this businesslike communication and peered closely into the envelope to see if any folding money was included.

"I wonder what the documents can be," Diana said, looking at the letter.

"Something to do with the government, no doubt," Miss Peabody assured her. "Very sensitive. I wonder who this Mrs. Whitby can be. I don't recognize the name. Very likely her husband works with Harrup at Whitehall. I shall be very happy to do it for him." Even though the letter was the only paper to be seen, Peabody still smiled.

"He might have asked his own servants to do it," Diana mentioned.

"His mama is not at home. He knows he can trust me to see the thing gets done."

"Why, Peabody, we shall be passing right through Hitchin ourselves tomorrow when we go to London to help Ronald settle in. We might as well pick up the documents and take them to Harrup," Diana pointed out. "He will get them more quickly that way. They're probably urgent."

Her chaperon knew by the twinkle in Diana's blue eyes that the minx was up to something. "Ha, you are a caution, Diana!" She smiled. "You are thinking that Ronald can come along when we take the documents to Harrup, and that will help his cause along."

"It won't do it any harm," Diana agreed.

"It is the very sort of special consideration Harrup likes." This came dangerously close to admitting Harrup was a tad high in the instep, and Miss Peabody quickly spoke on to remove the notion. "It does no harm to be polite to someone in Harrup's position. I'm sure he is so busy with meetings and Parliament and court that we must do whatever we can to help him." She carefully folded up the map and letter and put them in her sewing basket.

With a helpless look at Diana she said, "Would you

4

mind just nipping down and seeing Jennie isn't pouring bleach all over my best blue muslin? I told her to dilute it first. I swear the girl is either simple or ruins all the colored wash from spite. I'd go myself but my knees are stiff today. These spring winds are piercing."

"I was just about to go," Diana said.

After ascertaining that the blue muslin was unmarred by their fastidious servant, Jennie, Diana went upstairs to begin her packing. She and Peabody were remaining in London for only two nights, but Ronald might take them out to the theater, so she would take an evening outfit. She took from the clothespress her two favorites—a deep blue satin that matched her eyes and a less fancy but more comfortable gown of glossy gold lutestring, striped with narrow bands of green. With a last longing look at the blue, she returned it to the clothespress. Its décolletage was too elegant for the sort of evenings they would have with Ronald. That gown would be more at home at a ball.

The extremely disobliging Lord Harrup could take them to a ball if he chose. Miss Peabody followed his activities closely via her connections at the Hall and reported his vertiginous social whirl to Miss Beecham. With the season in progress, Harrup would be out waltzing and attending plays and operas every night. He was top of the trees, but in the usual way of toplofty gentlemen, he did not deign to invite his country neighbors to visit him in town. Diana knew she must be polite to him, though—for Ronald's sake.

She found being polite to Harrup one of life's less pleasant duties. A lordly neighbor who continued calling a young lady "missie" into her twenty-fifth year is not likely to inspire much affection. He ran quite tame at the Willows, taking potluck with her family three or four times for every invitation issued to Harrup Hall. But what really vexed her was that his invitations never coincided with the interesting parties at which he entertained his London friends. It was with the vicar and such local worthies that she and her papa were invited to dinner.

She put the lutestring dress on the bed and lay down beside it, looking up at the water marks on the ceiling. Seven of them, strung out like an archipelago right over her head, as unchanging as the continents and her life. They had been there, caught in plaster, turning from yellow to brown, for as long as she could remember. Would she go on looking at them all her life, turning dim along with them? Would she grow old and die here at the Willows?

Perhaps things would be different once Ronald got established in London. He was a brilliant scholar. He might advance swiftly at Whitehall. She fell into a delightful reverie in which Ronald was the mentor of cabinet ministers and kings, and she was his hostess—charming, well informed, suggesting a cabinet shuffle here, a war measure there, while fighting off the impassioned advances of half the government. Of course, it was all idle dreaming. She knew Ronald's scholarly mind wouldn't set Whitehall on fire. Ronald was the sort who would quietly and painstakingly do research for some more outgoing gentleman who would stand up and spout his words in the House and receive credit for them.

It didn't seem fair that a lady's hopes should ride on a younger brother whose social acumen was worse than mediocre. She was the firstborn; she should have been the man. Papa often said so himself. She was the better rider, the more spirited, the more venturesome of the two. She must bring Ronald into fashion somehow in London, when she finally got there. Ronald was only twenty-two—she felt a hundred. How had she got so old? Where had the years gone? Life was pleasant at the Willows with Papa and Miss Peabody, but it wasn't enough. There was no challenge in it for her. She had mastered the Willows and its limited society. She was the real ruler of the house. Diana longed to have a home of her own or a life of some sort beyond this provincial round of little doings.

She sighed and went to the mirror as she did at least once each day to check time's ravages on her face, for other than the five thousand from her mama, that face was her fortune. A broad brow tapered to full cheeks and a small, somewhat pointed chin. Her nose was straight and imperious, not at all matching her lopsided smile. Simple living had been easy on her charms. No trace of crow's feet encroached yet at the corners of her blue eyes. The eyes still wore the luster of youth, still tilted up at the outer rims. Her best feature. Surely those eyes were made for flirting over a fan, not for monitoring the application of bleach to the laundry. A pixie's eyes, Peabody called them. Her hair was pale blond and lightly curled. Gray wouldn't show in it easily.

Worrying about gray hairs, and she had never had a real beau yet! Just a few flirts like Mr. Henderson, who walked out with her two Sundays, then switched his affections to her friend Sukey Dunton. Diana hadn't even had the solace of a broken heart. It was half a relief when Mr. Henderson defected. The vicar smiled more warmly at her than at the other ladies on the church auxiliary. Dull little man with his dull little job. How did he stand it? How did any of them stand it, knowing there was a whole world out there to conquer? Ah, well, tomorrow she was going to London to help Ronald set up his apartment. Perhaps Ronald would introduce her to someone, one of his friends or associates. All she needed was one ambitious gentleman, and she would be on her way.

The trip to London was the subject of conversation over dinner, and when Mr. Beecham had retired to his office, Peabody went to her charge's room to see what she had packed, for they were leaving early in the morning.

"Not taking your blue satin, Diana?" she asked, lifting a brow.

7

"There's no point wrinkling it. I shan't need such a fancy gown, Peabody."

"Take it," Peabody advised, a twinkle in her dim eyes. "I'm taking my good black. There is no saying—Harrup might invite us to dinner."

Diana thought this extremely unlikely, but with a hopeful thought to Ronald's friends, she folded up the gown and added it, just in case.

Mr. Beecham saw them off early in the morning, counseling his groom what hotel to take the ladies to for lunch and where to bait the horses. Though Hitchin was ten miles away, Peabody already had Harrup's map on her knee when they left, considering the best route to the Whitby house. "Tilehouse Street," she said. "Yes, I know where that is. An excellent part of town. Salam Chapel is in Tilehouse Street."

John Groom had been instructed to keep a slow and steady pace. It was going on ninety minutes later that the carriage entered the old coaching town and proceeded past a smattering of picturesque houses to its destination. The Whitby residence proved to be more than genteel, a fine old stone mansion.

"We shall not accept tea, Diana, much as I would like a cup. We want to reach London before dark," Peabody said.

They stepped up to the door and were admitted by a butler. Peabody was a little surprised an M.P.'s man didn't wear livery, but a glance was enough to tell her the house was done up in the first style of elegance. Not a mote of dust to be detected by an eagle eye, which Miss Peabody's certainly was. As she waited in the saloon, the words *nouveau riche* occurred to her. Nothing in the chamber had been sanctified by age, but it was all so pretty that she decided to overlook its lack of ton.

Before long, Mrs. Whitby herself wafted in, and all thoughts of the room were forgotten. The lady was fine

8

enough to give ton to a hovel. Her age was hard to determine—Peabody pegged it in the vicinity of thirty. That rosy flush on the cheeks might be due to youth, but more likely to rouge. Hair as black and shiny as a raven's wing glinted with iridescent peacock tints in the window light. Peabody's experience with black dye in her younger years told her this fine color didn't come from a bottle. Dye made the hair a flat, mat black. The hair grew low on an ivory forehead. Large, limpid blue eyes were heavily fringed in lashes. Her nose was small and retroussé, and her lips were like rosebuds.

Diana made a swifter examination of the face and soon passed on to the toilette. An enviable morning gown of pale violet sarcenet encased a figure that bordered on the voluptuous while still maintaining the litheness of youth. Any hint that Mrs. Whitby was in half-mourning, however, was obliterated by her radiant smile and her décolletage. The smile turned quizzical when Mrs. Whitby beheld two unfamiliar provincials in her saloon.

Soon the name Lord Harrup was in the air, and the mystery was cleared up. "So if you have the documents ready, we shall take them and be off," Miss Peabody said.

"Ah, yes, the . . . documents," Mrs. Whitby said with a quizzing little smile. Something caused a wicked gleam to enter her eyes. She took a parcel from the table and handed it to Miss Peabody. "Give my kindest regards to Harrup, and tell him I shall look forward to seeing him soon in London. I find the country does not suit me. I can't sleep for the racket of the grass growing."

"I shall be happy to tell him," Miss Peabody answered, determined to be polite to any associate of Harrup's. "You stay in London when Mr. Whitby is sitting in the House, do you, Mrs. Whitby?" she asked conversationally.

"Oh, I am not married," Mrs. Whitby said. "I have been widowed forever. Are you visiting Harrup for long?"

9

Her eyes strayed to Diana, where they lingered, looking up and down for all the world like a forward gentleman.

"No, we are not visiting him at all, except to deliver these," Miss Peabody replied.

Mrs. Whitby opened her lips and a silver peal of laughter tinkled forth. "You must also tell him for me that I think he mistreats his lady friends, using them for errand boys. But then, that is Harrup's usual way, to abuse us ladies, *n'est-ce pas?*"

Miss Peabody felt her spine curl. "I'm sure Lord Harrup has always treated *me* with the utmost kindness," she answered firmly. "We are very happy to deliver these government documents for him."

Mrs. Whitby's lovely face looked blank. Then a look of understanding flashed in her eyes, and again she laughed, more merrily than before. "Of course. We are all eager to help Parliament—especially certain noble members thereof," she replied in a strangely insinuating tone.

On this peculiar speech she turned and flounced from the room without so much as saying good day.

"Peculiar woman," Miss Peabody exclaimed as soon as they were outside the door. "Why is she still in half-mourning if she has been widowed for eons? She hardly looks old enough to have been married long."

"Wasn't she beautiful?" Diana sighed. "I would *kill* for that gown. I'm sure she must have a French modiste. I liked her—a little brash, but lively."

"Handsome is as handsome does. Not even the courtesy to say good-bye. I cannot think Harrup will be overjoyed to see *that* one in London. I wonder what she was doing with these documents."

She settled into the carriage and glanced down at the packet of letters. They were held together with a pink satin ribbon. The scent of lavender was noticeable in the closed carriage. It was soon borne in on the Argus-eyed Peabody that she had seen the handwriting on the top envelope before, most recently yesterday when she received her letter from Harrup. She looked askance at Diana, who had already realized a pink satin ribbon sat uneasily on government documents. Neither did the envelopes look at all official. There were no seals on them but only Harrup's frank. Her eyes moved to the handwritten address and she gasped.

"Peabody!"

Peabody stuffed the letters into her reticule and snapped it shut. "Yes, Diana?" she asked blandly.

Her charge looked her in the eye and laughed aloud. "Too late. The damage is done. I've already seen Chuggie's handwriting. Good gracious, how shocking of you, taking me to visit a member of the muslin company."

Blood suffused Peabody's saturnine face, lending a livid hue to its usually sluggish complexion. She had leaped to the same conclusion a moment earlier and, for once in her life, was uncertain what posture to take. Rumors of Harrup's affairs had reached her ears before this. She had been able to overlook intimations of a bachelor's London peccadilloes, providing they remained rumors and remained based in London. To have pretty convincing evidence that the rumors were true and had strayed so close to Harrup Hall and the Willows was hard to digest. With no one else to take her ill humor out on, she turned on Miss Beecham.

"Fine talk for a lady! Muslin company, indeed! I think I know Harrup a little better than to believe he would give that trollop the time of day."

"Nonsense, she was a very elegant trollop, and why else would Harrup have written her so many letters if he weren't her lover? What I cannot understand is why he sent her to Hitchin to rusticate and listen to the grass grow. Peabody, let us see the letters." A look of genuine outrage leaped to Peabody's long face. "I don't mean read them. Let us just see how many and how thick they are."

"Certainly not," Peabody said firmly. But before the

11

carriage had gone ten yards, she decided she needed her handkerchief, which just happened to be under the letters so that she had to remove them. It wasn't her fault if the pink satin ribbon was a trifle loose and came off as soon as she tugged it a little.

A cascade of white squares fell to the carriage floor. Diana picked them up and placed them one by one in Peabody's lap. "Six," she said when she had finished. "I wonder how long he's been carrying on with her?" Diana narrowed her eyes as she contemplated this puzzle. "I noticed he's come home very often since winter. I wager that's when he made this liaison, in late winter or early spring. And now she's going to join him in London."

"Harrup always comes home often in the springtime. He and his bailiff have many meetings to decide about rotating crops and things. You know Harrup likes to oversee the planting at the Hall."

Undeceived, Diana continued this line of talk, which was so distasteful, yet exceedingly interesting to Peabody. "No, he took up with her at the end of January. You remember he darted home one afternoon and left for London that same night. He spent that night with Mrs. Whitby," Diana decided.

"He certainly did not. A courier arrived from Whitehall and called him back to an emergency meeting that weekend. It was the second week in March that it all started—that's when it was. He did not come home at all, but the vicar mentioned seeing him in Hitchin. That's when the hussy got her clutches into poor Harrup. That setup must have cost him an arm and a leg. Everything so expensive and brand new."

"And now he's taking her to London. I wonder if he'll use the same furnishings. Who can she be, Peabody?"

"Nobody," Peabody said angrily. She had finally found the villain in the piece. "You could tell by the bold eye in her head and the cut of that gown that she's as common as

12

dirt. An actress or some such thing—did you see the rouge smeared all over her cheeks? That one would as soon tie her garter in public as she'd sneeze. The very sort of creature that preys on innocent young men.''

"Harrup's thirty-five," Diana reminded her, and received a blistering stare for her foolishness. "I know all about his women, Peabody. His own mama complained to me last winter that she despaired of his ever marrying because he had his pick of all the prettiest lightskirts in town.''

Sixty-five years of Christian living prevented Peabody from opening the letters and reading them. Even sixty-five years couldn't stop her from analyzing the handwriting, the franks, smelling the scent of lavender at close range, and conjecturing wildly as to the current state of affairs. "Why is Harrup so eager to get his billets-doux back that he couldn't wait for his next visit?" she wondered aloud.

"This explains his wanting me to send one of the footmen from the Willows to Hitchin. He wished to keep the story away from his own home. There is something very odd here, Di.''

"Maybe he's broken off with her," Diana suggested, after a few moments' consideration.

This was balm to Peabody's spirit. "That's it!" she exclaimed. "He has given the hussy her congé—and I thank God for it. I wonder . . .''

"What?" Diana asked, with only mild interest. She was not so keen on Harrup's doings as her mentor. He was too highly placed to be a suitor to her, and too old to have featured as the hero of her girlish daydreams. As he never stirred a finger to introduce her to any of his eligible friends, he was out of mind as soon as he was out of sight. He had been a fully grown man for as long as she could remember, treating her as a mere youngster. When she thought of him, it was as a friend of her father's and Peabody's, and a neighbor who was more interesting than most by dint of his position as lord of Harrup Hall.

"Since he has had the sense to break off with that creature, I wonder if he is thinking of getting married. It is high time for it."

"That's probably it," Diana agreed.

"Who can the lady be?"

With such intriguing material to conjecture, the first lap of the trip passed quickly. Lunch was taken at the Red Lion in Welwyn, and there the conversation continued in their private parlor.

"Harrup will be embarrassed—that might be of some help when Ronald speaks to him about a position," Diana said. "I mean—well, he can hardly mount his high horse when he is looking so foolish, can he?"

"My dear, we must not let on we know a thing about these letters," Peabody exclaimed.

"Then we shall have to pretend we've suddenly become blind and stupid," Diana answered, laughing. "Now that we know what Mrs. Whitby is, I realize it was written all over her, and the love nest, too. Everything brand new, and good but not fine. Oh, you know what I mean."

"He doesn't know we were there."

"He'll know it the next time he speaks to Mrs. Whitby," Diana pointed out.

"I trust he has seen the last of her. We shall say we sent our own footman. And I'll wrap the letters in plain brown paper before I hand them over to him."

"Lying, Peabody? Tch, tch. I, for one, have every intention of ringing a good peal over Harrup."

Peabody pursed her lips and shook her head. "You are growing a little old to be still playing the hoyden with him, Di. It was all well and good to tease him and play off your tricks when you were a girl. Now he will expect better behavior from you."

Diana's smile showed that she did not mean to argue or

14

to give in. "Are you ready to leave?" she asked, glancing at her watch.

"Just let me freshen up. You can go and have the carriage called while I do it."

Diana went to the desk and sent for their carriage. Several clients were milling about the lobby, and servants carried dishes to and fro in the area of the private dining rooms. She glanced at the newspapers on the desk, waiting for Miss Peabody. The first notion she had that anything was wrong was a high-pitched scream from their parlor. She recognized her chaperon's voice at once and darted forward. If she hadn't known Peabody from her cradle days, she would scarcely have recognized the wraith holding on to the table for support. Peabody was as white as paper, wide-eyed and trembling.

Diana flew forward, calling, "Peabody! What's the matter? Are you ill?"

"Somebody stop him! Stop that man!" Peabody begged in a quavering voice. A shaking finger pointed to the lobby.

"What man? I didn't see anyone."

The manager came pelting in to add to the confusion. Peabody had soon recovered sufficiently to enlighten him and Diana. "A thief! My reticule has been stolen. Somebody go after him. A tall, dark young fellow."

"Which way did he go?" the manager asked.

"He didn't go out the front door. He turned the other way," Peabody said. "I watched him dart out. I was too overcome to give voice for a moment. One doesn't expect to be robbed in a respectable inn," she added blightingly.

They all ran into the hall. "The other way" wasn't much help. The man might have gone into the taproom, upstairs, to the kitchen, or out the back door. All these possibilities were investigated during the next few minutes. The other clients came forward to add their observations. One had seen a dark-haired young jackanapes peeking into the private parlor while Diana was glancing at the paper. He had

15

inquired of the clerk if a Miss Peabody or Miss Beecham had hired a parlor and asked which one. This was deemed highly suspicious. Another had seen him hurry out but hadn't seen the purse. Still another had thought the lad was fair, not dark. After a quarter of an hour it was clear that the thief had gotten clean away on a mount tethered just outside the inn door. While a rumpus was being raised within, he had mounted and pelted away like lightning. The only useful thing learned was that the man had headed off toward London.

Miss Peabody marched straight off to the constable's office to lay a charge. Constable Shackley agreed to take a ride down the London road, but by then the ladies knew they would never see the purse again, and Constable Shackley knew Miss Peabody's opinion of his sitting on his haunches while decent ladies were robbed of ten guineas.

"All our money gone," Diana moaned. What fun was London without money? "How shall we pay for our hotel? It nearly cleaned me out, paying for lunch and the change of team."

"That is not the worst of it," Peabody said. Her face was pinched with chagrin and her voice weak with guilt. "Harrup's letters were in my reticule. I have failed him."

"The letters! That's it!" Diana squealed. "You remember the clerk said someone was asking for our parlor. We thought it very odd at the time. He was after Harrup's billets-doux."

"Don't be ridiculous. How could anyone possibly know I had them in my reticule? It was our money he was after. I never can step foot outside the house without something dreadful happening. Ten guineas gone. How can I tell your papa?"

"Mrs. Whitby knew you had them," Diana countered, and stared at her chaperon with a sapient eye.

It did not take Peabody long to agree with this delightful

conclusion. Any possibility that the affair was still in progress was ended now. "I never did trust that sly blue eye in her head. But why would she agree to return Harrup's letters if she only meant to have them back?"

"She wouldn't incur his anger by refusing," Diana suggested. "But Mrs. Whitby has decided she shall be paid when she blackmails him with them."

Miss Peabody thought she was up to all the rigs, but the blackest idea that had occurred to her was that Mrs. Whitby wished to keep the letters for sentimental reasons, despite her sly blue eyes. A look of surprised admiration lit her face. "I believe you have hit it on it, Di. Was there ever such a piece of wickedness in Christendom? And how am I to tell Harrup about it?"

Diana patted her arm consolingly. "Don't worry about it, Peabody. *I* shall tell him," she said with quiet satisfaction. Peabody was groaning into her handkerchief and missed the expression that Diana wore. Had she seen it, she would no doubt have recognized it as being similar to Mrs. Whitby's conniving face.

Chapter Two

The fates conspired to heap more misery on Miss Peabody's trip. Roads were full of potholes that delayed their time abominably. A violent megrim took possession of her head, and just outside of London a buck forced their rig off the road in a game of hunt-the-squirrel. It took John Groom half an hour to haul the team out the ditch and make sure the carriage was sound enough to continue their journey. Informing Harrup of the loss of his letters was so urgent that she had the carriage driven straight to his house in Belgrave Square. In the lengthening shadows of twilight, stately brick homes glared down at their passing, like dowagers at a ball, stiffly disapproving of parvenues.

It was with a tremor of apprehension that Peabody lifted her hand and sounded the brass knocker. She didn't recognize Harrup's butler, who looked as imposing as a duke as he stared down his Turkish nose at them and announced in lofty accents that his lordship was not at home.

Peabody cast a stymied frown at Diana, who edged forward and said in a loud, clear voice, "We shall wait for him," and barged in.

"His lordship has left for the evening," Stoker informed her.

"I shall fall in a heap if I have to walk another step this night," Peabody moaned, and sank on to a chair in the hallway. While the butler looked on doubtfully, Diana took charge.

"Please prepare a chamber for Miss Peabody and myself," she said. "We shall spend the night here."

"But his lordship—" the butler began, and stopped uncertainly. His lordship had strong views on country cousins battening themselves on him uninvited. On the other hand, there was a certain fiery disdain in the young lady's eyes that Stoker knew did not glow in the eyes of commoners.

"Pray hurry," Diana said coolly. "Lord Harrup will not be happy to hear his cousin was kept cooling her heels when she came here at his express request."

"Yes, ma'am." This eased Stoker's mind, and he called for the housekeeper.

Mrs. Dunaway was only five feet tall, but she made up in bulk what she lacked in height. Plump and florid, she ruled the house with an iron fist. As the ladies were being shown upstairs by Mrs. Dunaway, Diana took a peek around her. The London house was, of course, smaller than Harrup Hall, but in elegance it was equally overpowering. Her eyes scanned the broad expanse of marble hallway leading to a gold saloon. Beyond a wide arch, lamps shone on polished mahogany surfaces and glowed dully on satin-covered sofas. The downstairs maid was just whisking the draperies closed.

Mrs. Dunaway, a cousin of Miss Peabody and a friend, chatted amiably as they ascended. Less charitable persons than Peabody said that Harrup demanded services of all his pensioners.

"His lordship will want you to have one of our good guest rooms, Hattie," Mrs. Dunaway said as she led Peabody down a carpeted hallway to a door eight feet high. When the tapers had been lit, the room was seen to be fit for a queen. Green velvet hangings at windows and on the canopied bed lent an air of being in a forest. The theme was picked up in the hand-blocked wall covering, where branches and leaves were intertwined against a cream background.

"Oh, my! I hardly think—" Peabody said, and glanced doubtfully at Diana. "But perhaps with Miss Beecham along to share the room with me—Harrup could not put her up in the servants' quarters."

"There's not another guest in the house at the moment," Mrs. Dunaway said. "We shall put Miss Beecham in the adjoining room. The beds are made up fresh, for we just this day got his maiden aunts from Bath bounced off. What a troublesome pair of barnacles they were. Methodists," she explained. "Now, will you ladies have a bite of dinner downstairs or shall I have it brought up here to you?"

"We would not want to inconvenience the servants. A cup of tea in our rooms will be fine," Peabody said modestly.

Diana remembered the countless times her papa's servants had been sent bustling when Harrup accepted a last-minute invitation to dinner. She was ready for more than a cup of tea. "When is Lord Harrup expected back?" she asked.

"He's dining with the lord chancellor, so should be home by ten. The Eldons, you know. Very dull little parties Old Bags gives. I know his lordship turned down all his invitations to routs later this evening. He is very busy in Parliament at the moment."

Diana considered this and took her decision. "You have your tea and go to bed, Peabody. I shall have a bite downstairs and wait for Harrup. I'll tell him what happened."

Peabody's face eased in relief at avoiding her unpleasant duty, and Mrs. Dunaway's eyes lit up like a pair of lamps at this tantalizing hint of trouble. As soon as she had Miss Beecham settled in the morning parlor with her cold mutton and bread, Mrs. Dunaway jiggled back upstairs to learn the details from Hattie Peabody.

"Mrs. Whitby, you say?" she asked, creasing her pink

brow. "No, she's not one of his city light-o'-loves. He's been carrying on with an opera dancer—nothing serious—but even that has dropped off. Now don't poker up, Hattie. He is a bachelor—and his females are all high-stepping dashers, nothing low class about them, I promise you. Lately it's all come to a halt. You'd think he was up for canonization the way he's burning the midnight oil. Work, work, work. You'd be proud of your Chuggie, Hattie."

"I was not proud of him this day, Agnes. To have such unsavory goings-on in front of Miss Beecham."

Mrs. Dunaway bit her lip and said, "The chit didn't seem overwhelmed by it all. She's not what you'd call a deb, I think? Older than seven."

"Older than that, but as green as grass. She's never been outside of the county, except for a few days in London with the family."

"Ah, well," Mrs. Dunaway replied, "country gels don't shock easy, as we well know, eh, Hattie?" On this comforting speech she trundled from the room to try her luck with Miss Beecham below. Two minutes in that young lady's company told her nothing but that—yes, it was unfortunate about the letters, and Miss Beecham would like to be informed the instant Harrup arrived. In the meanwhile she would like a pen and paper. Very cool was Miss Beecham for a chit who was supposed to be a provincial greenhead.

Over her coffee Diana wrote a note to Ronald, explaining that she had been delayed and would call on him tomorrow at his hotel. She then rang for a servant to deliver the message and resumed her wait. What she had seen of the house and servants impressed her. Harrup's dining with the lord chancellor impressed her. Her courage was beginning to fail, and she took herself firmly by the scruff of the neck. She would not apologize for barging in uninvited. It was Harrup's fault that they were in this pickle in the first place.

21

At ten-thirty Harrup's tread was heard in the hallway. Diana hastened to the door of the morning parlor but decided to wait and let Harrup come to her there. She listened impatiently as he handed his coat and hat to the butler.

"Anything happen while I was away?" Harrup asked. "I trust you got *Tantes* Gertrude and Millicent blasted off."

"Yes, milord."

"Good! Thank God for large favors. Bring me a very large brandy and my slippers to the study."

"You have company, milord," the butler murmured apologetically.

"At this hour of the night? Hell and damnation, who did you let in behind my back, Stoker?"

"A Miss Beecham and Miss Peabody."

"You know my views on harboring country neighbors."

"They said they were your cousins, sir. Here at your express request, the young lady said."

"She always was a forward wench, but this goes beyond anything. Why didn't they go to a hotel? Very well, where are they?" he demanded in a gruff voice.

"The young one's waiting for you in the morning parlor."

"Send for her. I'll be in my study. And bring the *bottle* of brandy, Stoker."

"Perhaps wine for the young lady, sir?"

"No, don't encourage them."

Upon hearing this rude speech and demeaning description of herself, Miss Beecham returned to the table. With a hand trembling in anger she poured herself an unwanted cup of coffee. When she was requested to follow Stoker, she smiled coolly. "Please send Lord Harrup to me. As you can see, I am not quite finished dinner. Thank you, Stoker."

"His lordship—"

"Immediately, if you please," she said, and speared him with a shot from her sharp eyes.

"Yes, Miss Beecham." Stoker bowed and returned to the study.

For some five minutes Diana waited, trying to catch a few words of the raised voice that shouted from the study. She was unconcernedly stirring her coffee when a stiff-legged Harrup finally entered the room. She had not often seen her country neighbor rigged out in city evening wear. He was an impressive sight. A tall gentleman, well built, with a crown of dark hair and dark eyes. Diana had no objection to a rugged face and weathered complexion. Were it not for the sardonic set of his mouth and the arrogant stride, one would have called him handsome.

Harrup looked as if he wanted to wring her neck, but he made the effort to appear civil. "Good evening, missie. What brings you to London?" he asked.

"Harrup." She nodded. "Pray join me and have some coffee. And don't feel obliged to apologize for not realizing I was still at the table," she added, meeting his glare with one of her own.

He strolled in and sat across from her. Lamplight flickered on his swarthy cheeks. "I didn't even realize you were in London. How should I have known you did me the honor of visiting me?" he asked.

Diana read the glint of anger in his eyes and prepared to set him down. "No doubt you are a little curious to learn why Peabody and I are here," she said.

"I am extremely curious."

"Curiosity has always been associated with cats—it seems it afflicts tomcats as well as females. Our visit has to do with your *chère amie*, Mrs. Whitby."

A spasm quivered at the back of his jaw. "I beg your pardon?" he asked haughtily.

"Well you might, when you hear what Peabody and I have been through this day. As if wandering into your ladybird's nest were not bad enough!"

Harrup jumped up from his seat. His eyes wore the look

23

of a man who is guilty all right, but hopes he might wiggle out unscathed. "What, if anything, are you talking about?" he demanded.

"Mrs. Whitby. It is for you to decide what, if anything, the name denotes."

Harrup stuck out his chin, straightened his cravat, and finally fell into a pelter, despite these delaying tactics. "Good God, you shouldn't have gone yourselves! I expressly told Peabody to send a footman."

"Yes," Diana snapped back. "And you expressly told us it was important documents that were to be picked up as well. What were we to think? We thought it had something to do with your work, and here it was only love letters to a lightskirt."

Harrup eased back onto his chair, considering whether he ought to be angry or apologetic. "A regrettable incident," he said, but his tone was not apologetic. "May I have the letters, please?"

"No, Harrup, you may not," Diana said, and stared at him with an expression he couldn't read, though he detected a trace of satisfaction in those bold, slanted eyes.

"Now see here, missie! I want those letters, and I want them now, with no tricks, or I'll turn you over my knee and give you a thrashing."

"Is that how a privy councillor treats a forward wench?" She smiled boldly. "I made sure more forceful measures were at your disposal—arrest, incarceration, deportation."

"Eavesdropping on top of it all! A thrashing is no more than you deserve, missie." Yet he felt foolish. The young lady before him, speaking adult English and looking at him with a woman's knowing eyes, was obviously too old to thrash.

"Very likely, but it wouldn't do you a bit of good. I don't have the letters."

Harrup frowned in confusion. "But I've already discussed

24

it with Laura. She agreed that five hundred pounds—'' He came to a self-conscious halt.

Diana's lips formed a mocking smile. "The wages of sin, though high, are not high enough to suit Mrs. Whitby. She wants more, it seems."

A quick frown furrowed his brow and his eyes narrowed dangerously. "Not another penny do I give. Did she actually have the gall to demand more money?"

"Not at all. She was charming—and very pretty, by the bye. I compliment you on your taste."

Harrup batted the compliment aside. "Then what happened? Where are the letters?"

"Peabody's reticule was stolen at the inn at Welwyn where we stopped for lunch."

Harrup continued frowning, but it was no longer an angry frown. He was rapidly conjecturing the likely outcome of this accident. "Pity."

"Yes, she had all our money in her reticule, which is why we are forced to seek rack and manger from you."

"Naturally I'll repay her. How much?"

"Ten guineas."

"Have you any idea who the thief was? What I am wondering is whether he'll realize the potential profit in what he picked up along with Peabody's purse."

Diana regarded him as though he were an idiot. "Peabody is the only one who saw the man, and she didn't recognize him. It was not done inadvertently by some simple cutpurse, however. The man asked specifically for our parlor. How did he know we were there? The only person who knew we had those letters and that we were en route to London was Mrs. Whitby. She sent him. The logical corollary is that she means to hit you up for more money."

Harrup's handsome features pinched in consternation as he considered this view. He looked a little pale around the jawline. "I can't believe it of Laura," he said. His voice was light with disbelief or disillusion.

"I daresay you'll believe it when you receive the demand for payment," she answered tartly. "How hot are the letters?"

"Plenty hot."

A little snigger of laughter escaped her lips, for it seemed so very droll to think of this stiff-rumped gentleman penning purple phrases to a lightskirt. "I'm surprised at you, Harrup. I thought you were up to all the rigs, and you behave like a Johnnie Raw. Ronald would not be so foolish as that."

"There was a reason," he defended reluctantly. "After moving Laura to Hitchin, I found I was able to spend very little time with her. To pacify her, I wrote from London occasionally."

"A bad investment all around. How did you come to take a mistress, and especially to move her out of town, when you were too busy to see her?"

"It's complicated," he said vaguely. "I moved her out of London because I was courting Lord Groden's daughter, Lady Selena. I am engaged, by the bye."

"Congratulations." Diana nodded. Her major interest in hearing this was to pass it along to Peabody. "Forgive my ignorance, but was it not an odd time to take up with a ladybird?"

"I had already taken up with her earlier. I only wanted to get her out of town."

"And as Lady Selena keeps you too busy to visit Hitchin, you were dropping Mrs. Whitby," Diana said.

"No, it's not Selena who keeps me so well occupied. The fact is, I am being considered for a very important appointment at court. Attorney general," he said, his chest swelling with pride. His chin lifted a little higher, and his face assumed that noble expression often seen on Roman statues.

"You—the conscience of the nation!" Diana exclaimed, and couldn't suppress a laugh.

26

The noble expression dwindled to annoyance. "That is the chancellor you're thinking of. I shan't be sitting on the woolsack till Eldon resigns—till he dies, actually. He has it for life. The attorney general is the first ministerial law officer of the government. A very important position. I want that appointment," Harrup added. His voice resonated with passion.

The Harrups had always been ambitious. Many such plums hung on the family tree, and as Harrup approached his peak years, he realized he was but little ornament to the family history. For that reason he had put his nose to the grindstone, his offer to Lady Selena, and decided to settle down. He was not accustomed to being thwarted in his desires, and a cold passion overcame him. He would do whatever he had to do to get that appointment.

"Does Mrs. Whitby know all this?" Diana asked.

"Of course; I told her." He rose and began pacing to and fro in the small room.

"A pity. You'll have to come down heavy for the letters."

Harrup's nostrils quivered in distaste, but no price was too high to pay for the attorney generalship. "I daresay," he agreed. "Probably five thousand guineas—something in that neighborhood."

Diana gasped at the sum. "Have you no gumption, Harrup?" she asked angrily. "You're going to be bled by a lightskirt! After setting her up in such high style, probably showering her with diamonds and giving her five hundred pounds besides, you're going to sit idly by while she demands more?"

"I can't allow any scandal at this time."

"No, gudgeon, but you can try to get your letters back."

Harrup blinked to hear himself described so bluntly but didn't object. "I don't see how. You don't even know who took them."

"Peabody got a look at the man," she reminded him.

27

"She'd recognize him if she saw him again. You know Peabody has eyes like a lynx."

"She's not likely to see him, is she?"

"He must have taken the letters back to Whitby. You'll have to break into her house. And furthermore, did you know she's coming to London soon? She told us to tell you she'd be seeing you here soon."

"I knew she was coming back. There's nothing for a woman like Mrs. Whitby in Hitchin."

"She'll bring the letters with her. She won't give them to you, but you can steal them."

Harrup stared in frustration and swore off an accomplished oath. "That wouldn't look good if I were caught— the aspirant to the position of attorney general breaking into a woman's house and stealing her letters."

"Reclaiming your letters—you've already paid for them."

"No, I can't risk it," he said after a brief consideration. "When I gave them to her, they ceased to be my property."

"Well, I can, and I shall."

"You?" he asked, and gave a dismissing smile. "Why should you put yourself to so much trouble?"

"Because I have a favor to ask of you. I shan't bother you with it now, but if I get the letters back, you must promise to give my request very generous consideration."

He leaned across the table and gave a satirical smile. "If you could get those letters back, my lass, I'd gladly buy you an abbey."

"You really do strike dreadful bargains, Harrup. Such largess as that is not a promise that will be kept. My request is more reasonable."

"Then just ask it. It's not necessary for you to pitch yourself into the fray. I shan't require a young lady to rescue me."

"I want to do it," she said simply. "I won't take any

28

foolish risks. Peabody and I shall look around town and see if we can find the thief. I expect he'll hold the letters till Mrs. Whitby comes to town. She said she'd be here soon.''

"It's worth a try,'' Harrup agreed. He thought the chances of success were very thin, but any chance was worth pursuing.

"This affair will take a few days,'' Diana said. "Can you lend Peabody and me some money? I mean above the ten pounds you're going to repay her. Hotels are so expensive, and there are the horses . . .''

"Stay here,'' he offered.

Diana looked up, startled. "You don't want provincials here, lowering the tone of your establishment.''

"My establishment's reputation is not so precarious as that. Stay. We want to be in close touch. I'll be more likely to learn who Laura's cohort is than you. I can finger the scoundrel and have Peabody identify him. My servants might be some help to you as well. Your father's groom won't be comfortable driving in London.''

"That's true,'' she said. "He allowed himself to be run off the road on the way here.''

Harrup's worried face softened in a smile. "Quite a day you've had, eh, missie? All my fault, and I apologize most humbly.''

"Quite a day, and as if to receive an extremely cool reception at the end of it weren't enough, you have to call me missie, as though I were a child. Actually, we didn't just come to London to deliver Whitby's love notes. Ronald is setting up an apartment, and we came to help him with the domestic details. I'll be seeing him tomorrow.''

"Invite him to meet you here,'' Harrup said at once. "It will be more comfortable than your visiting the Clarendon. Though it is the one spot in London where you can get a decent French dinner,'' he added consideringly

Diana didn't bother informing her host that Ronald was

not putting up at this famous and expensive spot. The economical Ibbetson's was the haunt of young graduates on the lookout for a position. "Thank you, I shall" is all she said.

"You'd best run along to bed now, Di. You look burnt to the socket."

She examined his worried face and realized how important the letters were to her friend. "So do you, Harrup."

"I have some government work to do before I retire. It's unfortunate I'm so busy. I'd like to show you around London. This is the first time you've visited me, I think?"

She gave him a jeering smile. "I got tired of waiting for an invitation and just came along uninvited."

Harrup looked abashed at this plain speaking. "Don't blush, Harrup. I'm quite familiar with your views on taking in provincial hangers-on and forward wenches."

"I'm sorry you overheard, but I see no reason to rescind the remark. My many relatives have taken the idea I run a hotel for their convenience, and then they have the nerve to complain if I take wine with my dinner."

"Neither Peabody nor I are at all Methodistical. It's not the serving of wine I object to, but the vintage. I had expected better than this at your table," she said, pointing to a carafe of decanted wine.

Harrup sniffed it and grimaced. "Kitchen wine. I'll speak to Stoker."

"You've singed the poor man's ears enough for one night. Let him be."

"Quite as presumptuous as my maiden aunts," he chided. "A guest should not undertake to order her host about. Country manners won't do in the city, you know. You must watch that tongue of yours."

Diana listened but heedlessly. "Is Lady Selena very proper, Harrup?"

"A pattern card of propriety, as becomes the attorney general's lady."

"Is that why you offered for her?"

"Only partly. She's also dashed pretty. She'd be snapped up inside of a month, so I moved quickly to secure her hand."

Diana bit her lip and wondered if she ought to air her fear. She figured Harrup was already in enough hot water without her adding to it. "Perhaps it's not a good idea for me to stay here. Lady Selena might dislike your harboring a young lady who is not a relative or anything."

He laughed it off. "Selena likes what I tell her to like. Besides, she'd have no reason to be jealous of you."

Diana felt a sting of anger at this unwitting insult. "I may not be so 'dashed pretty' as your fiancée, but that is no reason to dismiss me out of hand!"

"Good God, I didn't mean that!" he exclaimed. "You're like a little sister to me. We've known each other forever. Why, with Peabody having reared us both, we're practically siblings."

"You must be sure to tell Lady Selena that, so she'll know what to think," Diana snipped, and strode upstairs, tallying the insults she'd been subjected to that day. It was not the "forward wench" or the charge of country manners that hurt. That Lady Selena had no cause for jealousy was the one that settled in her heart.

Harrup went to his study and sat staring at the papers littering his desk. He wanted to be the attorney general so badly, he scarcely thought of anything else. All his life he had bought what he wanted—horses, houses, women. This was the first thing for which he had had to work and whose acquisition was in doubt, which increased his passion for it.

A vision of lovely Laura Whitby reared up in his mind. His fingers were clenched with the desire to encircle her white throat and squeeze. He could hardly believe such treachery from her. Those tears when he told her it was over between them—how sincere they had looked. Was it

31

possible someone other than Laura had got hold of the letters? Was it possible they were going to be published to thwart his hopes of getting the coveted appointment? A Whig trick, perhaps, to discredit him and the government?

But how could the Whigs know that Peabody had the letters? No, Laura must be at the bottom of it. Perhaps she'd taken a Whig lover and was being used without her own knowledge. That might be discovered at the House tomorrow. Harrup tried to work, but the problem continued to nudge at his attention, making work impossible. A pity little Missie Beecham had to stumble into this unsavory business. Not that it had shocked her much. She was growing up on him. Quite self-assured. She had acquired what his mama would call "countenance." How old would she be now? He remembered clearly the first time he'd seen her, a swaddled babe in her mother's arms. Funny little creature with a red, wrinkled face. She'd blossomed nicely, though. He'd been home from Eton on holiday that summer—ten years old? No, he must have been older. Di couldn't be twenty-four. But Ronald was younger, and he had graduated now. He wondered what Ronald had found for a job.

It was a night for worrying and remembering and thinking of the future. Harrup poured a large glass of brandy and drank it before he finally went up to bed. He had relived the past years of his life and envisaged a future that saw him as the prime minister of the country. Strangely, the dashed pretty Lady Selena did not once enter his mind.

Chapter Three

When Miss Peabody was apprised of the situation the next morning at eight o'clock, she decided to take breakfast with Mrs. Dunaway and the butler in the senior servants' kitchen. Any unpleasantness interfered with her digestion, and she feared Harrup would be unhappy that she'd discovered the truth about his "documents."

"Naturally, you, a guest, must dine with the family," she added to her charge. "Be sure to give dear Harrup my compliments. I shall see him at dinner this evening. Pray don't give him the notion he must come looking for me belowstairs to welcome me." This speech was interpreted to mean Peabody would be in alt if such a thing occurred.

Diana was happy to have privacy with her host. If Peabody were there, she'd be simpering and fawning over him. Harrup was already at the table when Diana arrived.

"Good morning. I had no idea you kept such early hours," she said. "I've been waiting in my room since seven-thirty. I didn't want to ring for tea, in case the servants were still asleep."

"You must request whatever you wish, when you wish it," he told her. "You are a guest in the house, not a servant."

"I'm glad you said that, Harrup, for I've been thinking over this problem, and there are a few things I shall need."

33

As she spoke, she helped herself generously to gammon and eggs from the huge silver serving dishes warming on the sideboard, and sat down.

"You have only to ask. Mrs. Dunaway will see to your needs."

"Not all of them, I think," she countered. "The thing is, Papa's traveling carriage is a wretched antique, so cumbersome for the city. As you are loaning me a groom, I wonder if you might throw in a carriage. Any old rig will do. Your curricle or, if you use it yourself, your regular city chaise will be fine. Except that my chaperon may not like the open carriage. You know how the wind always seeks out Peabody's ears. Let us say your city carriage," she decided.

The swift lift of Harrup's brows revealed his surprise at her presumption, but a second thought persuaded him. "I'm using the curricle these fine spring days, so my closed carriage is free," he agreed. "Where is Peabody? It's not like her to sleep in so late."

"She's eating with Dunaway and your butler. I believe she's a little shy to greet you, with the stolen letters hanging over her head. So foolish, as though it were in any way *her* fault. She said to say good morning. The thing is, I wonder if I should use Peabody for a chaperon in the city. Whoever stole your letters saw her, you see, and it might be a good idea if he didn't know that I'm associated with her. As he didn't see me, I'd like to remain unknown to him. If I manage to scrape an acquaintance, I shall call myself something else. In fact, as I'll be using an alias, you could tell Lady Selena I'm a country cousin. Just in case she decides to develop a mind of her own," she added pertly.

Harrup set down his fork impatiently. "Still smarting over that, I see. I must make clear at the beginning, I have no intention of embarking on a series of lies and subterfuges, missie. Neither do I intend to hire you a chaperon.

34

Don't go blowing this affair into a melodrama. You will not go near the thief who stole my letters.''

Diana blinked in confusion. ''How am I to recover them then?'' she asked.

''You're not,'' he said firmly. ''You can do one thing for me while you're here. I've been thinking about the problem, too, and it's fourpence to a groat the thief is a Whig. He's stolen the letters to embarrass me and the government. The likeliest place for Peabody to identify him is at the House today. He won't see you or her up in the visitors' balcony. Get Mrs. Dunaway to give you a pair of opera glasses, tell me where he's sitting and his name, if it happens to come up. I'll handle it from there.''

''Is that all?'' she asked. Her face fell in disappointment. Diana had been envisaging a delightful escapade of following the villain, possibly having Ronald accost him in a dark alley, preferably with the aid of a pistol. Even a surreptitious trip into the thief's house to steal back the letters had occurred to her. To have her role reduced to sitting in a balcony while Peabody fingered the culprit was hard to accept.

''That's all,'' he said. ''Leave a note at my office at Westminster if the culprit is recognized. I shan't be home till early evening.''

''Oh, very well.'' She sighed.

Harrup looked at her drooping shoulders and felt a stab of pity. ''You think I'm a spoilsport. Don't waste your trip worrying about my little problem,'' he said heartily. ''You and Peabody do what you have to do to get Ronald settled in, then go shopping. I have Peabody's money here,'' he added, handing her an envelope. ''The portion above ten pounds is a gift. Peabody will understand.''

''Thank you, Harrup,'' she said politely. It didn't seem the proper moment to mention her favor. She had hoped Ronald could walk in and hand him the letters. That would have been the time to hit him up for a job.

Harrup finished his coffee and rose to leave. "You won't forget to see Peabody before you go?" she mentioned. "She's with Mrs. Dunaway belowstairs."

"I'll see her later. I'm in a hurry this morning," he replied, pulling out his watch.

"Harrup!" she exclaimed. "Really! You can't spare two minutes for your old nanny? It would make her day. She especially asked me to tell you *not* to go to her, and you know what that means."

"You give her the envelope," he said.

"It's not the money. She wants the glory of your going after her in front of your city servants."

"You're insane," Harrup said, and strode from the room.

Diana was annoyed with him, but as she sipped her coffee, she supposed a man in his position was too busy to patronize a mere servant; Peabody's connection to Harrup was extremely tenuous. She spent half an hour wandering through the house, admiring much and mentally placing the "dashed pretty" Lady Selena amid the finery. With no real knowledge to go on, she pictured someone like Mrs. Whitby, only younger and haughtier. It must be nice to be Lady Selena, the prettiest deb of the year, nabbing an excellent *parti*, to be mistress of this house and Harrup Hall.

At ten she went and told Peabody what was expected of them. "Harrup said to take opera glasses. The ladies' balcony must be up under the eaves. Oh, and he said to give you this money. Your ten pounds and a little gift."

Peabody's face was wreathed in smiles when she peeked into the envelope. "Dear Chuggie—so generous. I knew how it would be. He told me when he came to see me that you would tell me what we are to do. He was in a great rush, but he found time to say hello before leaving. Agnes and Stoker were shocked. And he won't hear of our going to a hotel, you say. Just like him."

Diana showed all the astonishment the occasion demanded, but her smile was for her own triumph. He had taken her advice, after all. "We're taking his carriage," Diana said.

It didn't seem possible Peabody's smile could grow broader, but it did. "He thinks of everything," she said.

Diana didn't bother telling her chaperon how the carriage came to be offered. "After we go to the Upper House, let us call on Ronald. Harrup said we could invite him here, but I wrote him last night that we'd call at his hotel, so we'll do it."

"Invite Ronald here? So obliging!" she cooed.

Peabody had many compliments on Harrup's chaise as they spun along to Parliament. "How smoothly it glides. Exceptionally well sprung." Neither lady mentioned that the superior roads of London might have anything to do with it.

Peabody's more customary voice of complaint did not arise till she viewed the staircase to the visitors' gallery at Westminster. "I'm not at all sure I can tackle that climb, Diana. My knees always seize up on me when I travel. It's the wind seeping into the carriage that does the mischief. Your papa's carriage, I mean. Had it not been for Harrup's excellent goosefeather tick, I wouldn't have got a wink of sleep."

"Lean on my arm," Diana said, and began hauling her chaperon up the long, narrow flight.

The visitors' gallery was deserted at that early hour of the day, as were most of the seats in the House of Lords. The ladies looked down with interest at the chamber of the House, to see where the country's business was transacted. The monarch's empty throne was scanned by Peabody's glasses. In front of it sat the lord chancellor on his red woolsack, wearing a great gray wig. Rows of benches upholstered in scarlet rose in tiers on either side of the rectangular room.

"So this is where they keep raising our taxes," Peabody said. "Very grand, I'm sure. Where is Chuggie sitting?"

He was discovered bent over his desk, and Peabody smiled as proudly as though he were the fruit of her own womb.

"Harrup suspects the thief was a Whig. He should be sitting on the lord chancellor's left side," Diana informed her.

Within five minutes Peabody had run the opera glasses over the slender gathering and informed Diana that the villain was not present. As she spoke, two more robed gentlemen entered and took up their positions. Peabody studied them carefully but didn't recognize either one.

"Try the other side," Diana suggested.

Their villain was not to be seen there, either, but gentlemen kept straggling in, so the ladies sat on, carefully observing each newcomer. A very tedious morning was spent in this fruitless manner. At a quarter to twelve, Peabody could take no more.

"He's not here," she said. "I cannot sit in this stifling, airless little attic a moment longer, Diana. My ears are buzzing. Let us go and see Ronald."

"Very well, but I should send a note around to Harrup's office first. I told him I would."

She wrote her note and went in search of either Harrup's office or someone to deliver the note for her. In a corridor they met a page boy. Diana was just handing him her note when she felt a tugging on her elbow. Turning, she saw Peabody's jaw clenched in alarm. Her chaperon was ducking her head to remain unseen, and her finger was pointing at a man who was approaching them. Diana looked quickly as the man bustled past, his head buried in a letter. She saw a young man of average height and build. He had chestnut hair and a nondescript but not displeasing face.

"That's him," Peabody gasped.

"Are you sure?"

"I'll never forget his bold face as long as I live."

Diana felt a thrill of triumph. She said to the clerk, "Did you recognize that man? I think I've seen him somewhere before."

"That's Viscount Markwell, old Lord Belvoir's son and heir. A bright young lad. He's working with Lord Eldon's office."

"Yes, I thought so. About my note—would you mind waiting a moment? I just remembered something I must add." She hastily scribbled down the gentlemen's name and sent it off to Harrup.

"That's that," Peabody said happily as they went to the carriage to proceed to Ronald's hotel. "I am very happy to be able to help Chuggie. A morning in that dreadful aerie was well worth it. I hope I haven't taken one of my chills."

"Yes," Diana agreed, but a frown creased her brow. Harrup had thought the man must be a Whig. Why would a fellow Tory want to embarrass his own party? The man worked with Eldon, besides—he must be a friend of Harrup's. "Are you quite sure that was the man, Peabody?"

"Positive. The same eyes, a ginger shade, and that little lock of hair falling over his forehead. He'd had his hair cut. It wasn't quite so short over the ears before, but it is the same person, I promise you."

Perhaps Harrup could make some sense of it. Diana's part in the mystery was over, and she turned her mind to Ronald. He was waiting in front of the hotel for them, pacing up and down the street. As the street was empty, he didn't bump into anyone. His papa often said his son couldn't cross a desert without knocking something over. Ronald was a slender but elegant figure. He was prey to no freakish excesses of fashion. His jacket of blue Bath cloth was well cut, the buttons not ostentatiously large or yet too small for the current mode. His waistcoat was a discreet beige, his Hessians polished to a city sheen. He lifted his curled beaver when he saw them, revealing hair like an infant's, fine as silk and the color of sand, slightly curled. Ronald always managed to be pale, whatever his health or whatever the weather. What could be expected, when he stayed up too late and remained too much indoors reading? Constant reading gave his young eyes a fatigued look, and his habitual expression was one of irresolution, but his smile was sweet and gentle, his whole desire to please as he hastened forward.

"Diana, Peabody! At last you've come. I've been pacing up and down this street since nine o'clock this morning. What kept you?"

"I'll tell you all about it, Ronald," his sister replied. "Why on earth did you not wait for us in your room? We would have asked for you."

"I thought you might not like to go into a hotel alone," he said vaguely. As he helped Diana from the carriage, he managed to knock her bonnet askew.

"Good gracious, we may be provincials but we're not that backward! Is there somewhere we can go and sit down? I expect Peabody would like her tea," Diana said.

Ronald offered a hand to Peabody, who was swift enough to escape his help and reach the road unharmed. "We could go into Ibbetson's," he mentioned. "Or to my place. I haven't found a servant yet, but I am to pick up the key to my flat this morning. At ten-thirty, actually," he added, pulling out his watch.

"In that case, you'd better get into the carriage at once," Diana said. "You're nearly two hours late."

Ronald directed the driver to the real estate office and thence to his rooms. During the trip, Diana informed him of their adventures since leaving the Willows. "As Homer said, 'There is no more trusting in women.' I doubt there ever was," Ronald said morosely.

He was extremely dismayed, nor could he see any possible advantage to himself in helping Harrup.

"Have you tried to be in touch with Harrup at all?" Diana asked.

Shy and retiring, Ronald would as soon walk into Exeter Exchange and bite the tiger as ask a favor of anyone. Harrup, in particular, always made him feel as if his jacket was too small and his hair badly cut. "I didn't like to pester him at home about a job, you know," he said. "A man likes to take his ease at home."

"Oh, you went to his office."

His pale face looked diffident. "He would be so busy at the House that I didn't think I ought to accost him there."

"Where on earth did you plan to visit him, then?" Diana asked, becoming impatient with his shilly-shallying way of going on. "The middle of the street is hardly the place for it."

"Now that you are staying with him, it will be unexceptionable for me to call at his home," he decided.

Diana shook her head. "Ronald, I despair of you. You'll have to be thicker-skinned than this to get on in the world. You're too modest."

"Pride is the vice of fools, Di. I hope I am not a fool."

His sister thought he had certainly not been proud in hiring himself accommodations. The rooms were neither large nor elegant, but they were at least conveniently located on a side street off Whitehall, with a view of the Thames from one window.

Peabody strode from room to room, disparaging everything. "You'll get an ague with that wind blowing off the river. Be sure to stuff your ears with cotton wool, Ronald. My, would you look at the filth of this place! A pack of gypsies is what's been camping here. This boot box won't hold your books, Ronald, let alone a desk and lamp. And look at the state of these furnishings. They haven't seen a dust cloth this decade. We have our afternoon's work cut out for us, Di."

Diana was familiar with Peabody's love of overseeing

work being done by others and had no intention of spending her day polishing furniture. "Yes, indeed, we must find Ronald a servant. Do you prefer a man who could act as valet, too, Ron, or would you rather have a woman-of-all-work? She would cook and wash for you, but you'd have no help in dressing."

"Well," Ronald said uncertainly. "It would be nice not to have to go out to eat every day. On the other hand, I don't want to be unquiet, having a woman forever dusting and polishing when I'm trying to work."

"You needn't fear London servants will disturb you unduly in that way," Peabody said.

"Servants only come in two sexes," Diana pointed out. "A woman, I think. We'll go to an employment agency and have some sent along to be interviewed. We have a trunk of things at Harrup's place. Peabody packed linens and candles, and I don't know what all."

"That was kind of you, Peabody." He smiled gently. "I wish I could fine someone just like you to take care of me and make my little house a home."

Peabody's face melted in joy. "What would they ever do without me at the Willows?" she asked. "Cook would poison your papa with burned meat and raw fruit—and as to that lazy Jennie who does the washing!"

"We could not possibly give up Peabody," Diana informed her brother.

"I wasn't suggesting stealing Peabody!" Ronald said, shocked that such a charge should be hurled at him. "Someone *like* Peabody is what I said."

"There is no one else like Peabody," Diana said. "Let us go and see what we can find. But first let us have some lunch."

Peabody gave a warm, watery smile. "While we eat, we'll send Harrup's carriage back to Belgrave Square and have Ronald's trunk brought here. I shall settle him in. I'll make up your bed, Ronald, and tidy things up here just as you like, with plenty of candles.''

The remainder of the day was taken up in hiring a servant, shopping, and making Ronald's rooms comfortable.

"I don't know what I would have done without you,'' he said when the job was done. "Miss Rankin seems a very decent sort of woman. I especially like that she won't be sleeping here. I'll be out all day at work, and she can cook dinner and leave me in peace at night. It will be almost as good as not having her around at all," he said happily.

"Mind you, keep an eye on her housekeeping accounts,'' Peabody cautioned. "She'll be taking home more food than she serves you if you don't watch her. Snatching up half-burned candles, too—they're all alike, these servants.''

"It's six o'clock,'' Diana said. "What would you like to do this evening, Ronald?''

"We'll have dinner somewhere first. There are all sorts of amusements to see afterwards—plays and concerts.''

"Not for me,'' Peabody said. "I promised Harrup I would see him this evening. You youngsters go along and enjoy yourselves.''

"I must go back to Harrup's place and change,'' Diana said. "Why don't you change now and come along with us, Ronald? It will be a chance to speak to Harrup about finding you a job.''

"Very well,'' he said, but reluctantly.

Ronald was vastly relieved that Harrup was not in evidence when they reached Belgrave Square. He had been detained at Westminster but was expected home shortly. The servants were all abustle preparing a dinner party.

"Lord and Lady Groden and their daughter, Lady Selena, are coming,'' Mrs. Dunaway told them. "It's a small party, a family dinner you might say.''

"I shall dine with you and Stoker, Agnes,'' Mrs. Peabody decided. Though she'd sooner lose an arm than admit it, she was not entirely comfortable dining with Chuggie, and to do so in the presence of another whole noble family gave her palpitations even to consider it.

"And you, Miss Beecham? Will you and your brother be dining with his lordship?" Mrs. Dunaway asked.

"No, we are dining out."

"That is a pity. It would make some young company for Lady Selena if you could stay," the housekeeper mentioned.

Diana looked surprised. "I cannot think she will want any other company when she has her fiancé!"

"With old Lord Groden here, the table talk will degenerate into politics. That's all they ever talk of. Not much fun for a young lady."

"Then the young lady should introduce some other topic," Diana suggested.

Mrs. Dunaway took Peabody and Ronald to her parlor for a glass of wine while Diana dressed. The blue satin was left on its hanger. It was the lutestring she meant to wear. It had been decided that Ronald would take her to Drury Lane to see Sheridan's *The School for Scandal*. Diana was accustomed to dressing herself and doing her own hair. She was no peacock where fashion was concerned, but she took special pains with her toilette that evening. She piled her golden curls high on her head and attached her diamond-and-pearl earrings. Anticipation of the evening lent a flush to her cheeks and a sparkle to her blue eyes. Her evening cloak of embroidered silk with a small collar of sable was considered all the crack at home, and while she didn't expect to turn any heads at Drury Lane, she didn't want to look a dowd either.

When she was ready, she went to the staircase and looked down. What a fine house Harrup had. The chandelier cast reflections of dancing rainbows on the marble floor below. On a side table a large bouquet of flowers at, bringing a welcome touch of nature to the formal elegance all around. In her second-best evening attire, Diana felt like a duchess about to descend to a ball—except that no admiring cavalier stood below, waiting for her. She put her hand on the brass railing and went down slowly, lifting her skirt to prevent tripping.

When she was halfway down, the front door opened and Harrup entered, still in his blue jacket and fawn trousers. His brows were drawn together in a frown, making him look angry. When he glanced up and saw Diana, his brow cleared, and a smile lifted his lips. He stood at the bottom watching her descent, then held out his hand to greet her.

"What an enchanting welcome! I'm more accustomed to being greeted by Stoker's glower or Mrs. Dunaway's portly presence."

"And had your scowl in place to welcome them. Good evening, Harrup. Did you receive my note?" she asked. At this close range, she saw the fine lines on his forehead, the tired look about his eyes.

"I did. Why are you wearing a cloak, Di? You cannot be leaving so close to the dinner hour."

"I am dining out this evening."

"Nabbed a beau that quickly, did you?" he teased.

"No, a brother. Ronald is taking me to Drury Lane after dinner. About my note, Harrup—"

"Shall we go into my office? I haven't much time. Selena should be arriving within a half hour, and I still have to change." He accompanied her to his office and pointed to a chair, but she remained standing.

"Did you speak to Lord Markwell?" she asked.

Harrup just shook his head. "There's some mistake here. Markwell couldn't possibly be the man who took my letters. He's a colleague and friend of mine. He worked with Eldon and myself on several bills that are before the House. He'd be as horrified as I am to learn of my predicament. Of course, I haven't mentioned the matter to anyone yet."

"Peabody was certain," Diana said. She began to pace the office. Her shoulders were straight, and her long cloak fell gracefully to the floor. With her golden hair gleaming, she looked almost regal as she walked to and fro. Harrup watched her with interest, vaguely wondering when Di had become so grown up, so elegant. "She even noticed he'd had a haircut," Diana said. "It must be Markwell. Perhaps Mrs. Whitby put him up to it. Did he know you were severing connections with her?"

"Of course he knew. We work together every day."

"Did you work together yesterday, at around noon? If he was with you at that time, Peabody is obviously wrong," she pointed out.

Harrup drew his brows together in the familiar frown. "No, he was with his family in the country—his father is ill. He left Friday evening and only came back this morning."

Diana cast a sapient eye on her companion. "That gives him plenty of time to have gone to Hitchin and arranged matters with Mrs. Whitby."

"But why would he do such a thing? It doesn't make any sense—unless, as you say, he did it for Laura."

"Harrup, if *you* do not get the appointment, who does?"

"One of Eldon's other assistants. Walters or . . . or Markwell," he said, and looked at Diana's knowing smile. He rubbed his chin and began pacing alongside Diana. "Actually, Walters isn't pushing for the post. He's going on sixty-five, more interested in cutting back than forging ahead."

"There you are," she said triumphantly. "That's his motive, to discredit *you* so *he* becomes the attorney general. The strongest motive in the world—self-advancement."

"I must be growing old. There was a time when that speech would have sounded absurd to me. I do believe you're right, though. Self-advancement has taken the front seat,'' Harrup said. He continued mulling the matter over. ''Markwell's as ambitious as anyone. And he knew where I set Laura up. He's met her a few times, too, at Vauxhall one evening and at a few parties.''

Diana stared. ''Harrup, do you mean to say you take that woman into polite company?''

''No, into the other sort of company. Vauxhall is not exactly respectable. In any case, that was before my betrothal.'' At these words, he remembered Lady Selena was to arrive soon and glanced at his watch.

''You must go and change,'' Diana said. ''But before you go, could you tell me where Markwell lives?''

''I don't remember exactly. Since his father has become ill, they rented the family mansion in Grosvenor Square, and Harold has taken rooms somewhere.''

''Don't you have a list of addresses of the members of Parliament—something like that?''

''I seem to remember they issued one a few months ago. They're forever showering us with paper. I don't recall what I did with it, or whether I even kept it. It might be in that pile,'' he said, nodding toward his desk, where paper mounted a foot into the air. Suddenly suspicious, he asked, ''Why do you want to know?''

''We'll have to get into his rooms and look for the letters,'' she explained.

Harrup heaved a heavy sigh. ''I'll take care of it, Di. I don't want you arrested for burglary. Your papa might take it amiss. When you are in my home, you're under my protection.''

She slanted a pixie smile at him. ''Do be sensible, Harrup. How could I burgle Markwell's house when I was under your roof? Naturally, I shall have to escape your protection to do it.''

''Naturally, but you will do nothing about it till I have spoken to Harold.''

47

"He will hardly admit it!" she exclaimed, astonished at his naïveté.

She watched, entranced, as Harrup's fingers curled into fists and his complexion darkened amazingly. "Will he not?" he asked in a voice as soft as silk and as dangerous as gunpowder.

"Violence is not the answer," she warned. "Markwell is a sneak thief, and it is sneak thievery that should be employed against him."

"It's no job for a lady. I'll handle it. You just go and enjoy the play."

Diana smiled, as though agreeing. "I'll speak to you later, when I return."

"Must you go out? I wanted you to meet my fiancée." He ran an eye over her. "Though now that I see you all rigged up to the nines, I begin to appreciate your warning. Selena might well take exception to such stiff competition."

"Why, thank you, Harrup. That skates dangerously close to being a compliment."

"If you had met Selena, you would realize it is a compliment of the highest order." A bemused, faraway light glowed in his eye as he considered his lady.

"An incomparable, is she?"

"Naturally. A man's wife is an ornament and a criterion for judging his taste. Could you doubt I chose the most beautiful deb in town?"

She gave him a long look. "Is that your definition of a wife? She sounds more like a diamond tiepin."

He smiled reluctantly. "A diamond of the first water, but thus far I haven't found a diamond that can give me a son and heir."

"You *do* allow that the ornament has one useful function, do you? To reproduce a likeness of yourself."

Harrup lifted a brow, warning Diana that he was trying to be shocking. "She has two useful functions outside of being ornamental. She must not only produce a son but give some pleasure in the doing.''

She just leveled a cool look at him. "I thought the Mrs. Whitbys of the world handled that latter function."

"I've failed to shock you. I see the bloom is off the country rose. Perhaps it's just as well you aren't dining with Selena.''

"Don't tell me you're marrying a Bath miss!" she exclaimed. "I made sure you would choose a lady who is up to all the rigs.''

"No, for marrying, a man chooses the other sort," he replied, and strode from the office.

Diana began sorting through the pile of papers. Finding nothing useful, she pulled open his drawers and rooted there. She discovered the address list buried beneath a pile of personal letters. The letters were pulled together with a piece of string and labeled "Mrs. Somers." A glance at the dainty script and a whiff of rose water told Diana they were from a ladybird. She shook her head in dismay. The man was incorrigible. She copied down Markwell's address and stuffed it into her purse. Just as she was returning the list, Harrup appeared, outfitted now in black jacket and pantaloons and looking fine as a star.

"I found the address list," she said.

Harrup looked at the drawer and then looked a question at Diana. "What else? You aren't breathing through your nose for sheer joy.''

She tossed her head. "If you have to come down too heavy for Whitby's letters, you might recoup the loss by blackmailing Mrs. Somers," she snipped. "I notice you kept her billets-doux."

He went to the drawer, took the packet of letters, and dropped them into the wastebasket.

"It would be more to the point to burn them," she said. "Does Mrs. Somers also have a packet of your maudlin ramblings?''

49

"No, it is the custom to exchange letters when the affair is over. That ensures their safety. It happened that Mrs. Somers went abroad without retrieving hers, though I had the foresight to recover mine."

"Did you return Mrs. Whitby's?"

"Of course." Diana sniffed and tossed her shoulders. "As all this is so distasteful to you, why do you persist in helping me?" he asked.

"I told you, I have a favor to ask. But Lady Selena will be here shortly, and besides, I want you in a good mood, so I shall wait till tomorrow. Another little worry for you, wondering what you will be dunned for," she quizzed.

"I have enough worries, thank you. The attorney generalship hanging in the balance, the stolen letters, and Lady Selena."

"Lady Selena! I didn't realize she rated as a problem."

Harrup looked conscious and spoke quickly. "Marriage is always a problem. It's an institution designed by ladies to make slaves of men."

"It has often occurred to me that it is quite the reverse. It is the ladies who take on the responsibility of running the house and servants and making sure the husband isn't bothered by the children or any domestic problem. You cannot even complain of the expense. I expect you'll be getting a fat dowry with your bride."

"Naturally I was not speaking about Selena, but about marriage in general," he said stiffly.

She gave him a look that went right through him. "Naturally," she said. "Why are you *really* getting shackled, Harrup? Is it a prerequisite to the appointment you're hoping for?"

"Certainly not, though Liverpool did drop me the hint a married man is considered more stable, less likely to be running wild."

"I doubt if it will stop you. I suggest you take the precaution of keeping your desk drawer locked after the nuptials.''

The sound of carriage wheels was heard on the street, and Diana left. She went after Ronald, and rather than interrupt the arrival of Harrup's guests by going out the front door, they left by the servants' entrance.

"Ronald," Diana said when they were seated in the carriage, "we aren't going to Drury Lane, after all."

"I'm sure we can get a ticket. It may not be a very good seat, but—would you rather go to Covent Garden?"

"No, I would rather recover Harrup's letters. I have got Lord Markwell's address. Evening is the perfect time to sneak into his apartment and steal them."

Ronald turned and laughed lightly. "You are always joking, Di. What the deuce are you talking about, breaking into a gentleman's home?"

"Lord Markwell is not a gentleman. He is a thief."

Ronald realized by the timbre of his sister's voice that she was serious. A cold sweat broke out across his shoulders and along his forehead. A quotation drifted through his mind—he couldn't remember the author. "There is no animal more invincible than woman." "Oh, dear," he said softly. "Must we?"

"Yes, we must, for Harrup has taken the perfectly corkbrained idea of beating Markwell up, and that won't do his chances of being appointed the attorney general much good. If, on the other hand, you pull him out of the suds, he might just appoint you his special assistant."

"Aristophanes," Ronald murmured.

"What?"

"Nothing. Special assistant, did you say?" Ronald asked joyfully. "By jove, that'd be something like. Cuthbert got himself taken on as Lord Worth's assistant, and Worth is just a plain M.P., not even a privy councillor."

"It's just an idea," Diana warned him, "but this is very

important to Harrup, and he can be generous when he wants.''

"Let's see the address," Ronald said eagerly.

"Let us have dinner first. We must lay plans."

Chapter Four

"How many servants is a man like Markwell apt to have?" Diana asked her brother as they ate dinner. It was only an indifferent meal. Neither was in the mood for a lingering repast in some fine dining spot. They wanted to get on with the job at hand, so settled for Ronald's former hotel, Ibbetson's.

"A gentleman in his position would have to keep up a good front. He'd have about two thousand a year from his papa. I'd say two or three servants: a valet and butler, or a valet who also buttles and a female to look after his rooms and do a bit of cooking. As he has only hired rooms, his female servant may sleep elsewhere, like my Rankin."

"If Markwell makes do with one man, then we should have no trouble," Diana ventured. "I'll knock on the door and distract him while you rifle the office. I shall say I felt faint and ask for a glass of wine. Perhaps I should send him for a doctor," she mused, thinking aloud.

"What if Markwell is at home himself?" Ronald asked.

"Then we shall have to wait till he leaves. Surely he won't be home at this hour. I've heard Harrup say a bachelor in London can eat out every night of the week if he possesses an impeccable jacket and a passable reputation."

Ronald nodded his agreement. "Even I have had several invitations already," he mentioned.

"Why do you say *even* you, Ronald?" she asked angrily. "You speak as though there were something the matter with you."

"I ain't exactly a catch," he mumbled.

"Why, you're handsome, well educated, wellborn, and have an unsullied character. You have good prospects—you'll be the owner of the Willows one day. And soon Harrup will be your patron," she added, smiling.

Ronald look mystified at his lack of social success. "I don't seem to add much to a party," he said.

"You must learn to put yourself forward more forcefully. Keep your eyes open for any chance of advancement. And when you begin looking about for a wife, Ronald, you should bear in mind your own reticence and seek someone who is outgoing, who will be a help to your social life."

"That sounds like you, Di," he pointed out.

"I should be very happy to play your hostess till you marry," she agreed.

"That might be forever. I turn into a *blanc-manger* when confronted with a bold woman," he said, and mildly ate up his meat.

When the carriage delivered them to Glasshouse Street, Ronald looked around with interest. "That's the place," Diana said, pointing to a mansion halfway between Old Bond and Swallow that had been turned into four bachelor flats.

"I thought it might be," he said. "I was with Cuthbert when he was looking at one of those flats, but they were too steep for him."

"You wouldn't know which one was Markwell's?" Di asked.

"No, but the two on the top floor were still to let last week, so he must be on the ground floor. They're dandy rooms, light and airy. Cuthbert was going to try to raise the wind to hire one."

"Excellent! If Markwell is on the ground floor, we can

peek in the windows and see if he's home. I'll recognize him and know if it is the right flat.''

This subterfuge proved unnecessary, though a few other precautions were taken. Diana had Harrup's carriage wait in the shadows a block away, lest anyone recognize the crest blazoned on the panel. She and Ronald walked past the building twice, then went to the front door. In the entranceway, they found a small white card had been posted listing the occupants. Lord Markwell occupied the set of rooms to the left of the entrance passage.

"There were no lights burning in those rooms," Diana whispered. "Do you think you could pry the lock open?"

Ronald looked lost. "How?" he asked blankly.

"I don't know. With a clasp knife or whatever men carry."

"I don't carry a clasp knife. I have a patent pen, and a small magnifying glass—for looking at old books at the stalls, you know. Sometimes the print is blurred and rather hard to read. I'll just knock at the door—in case someone is in there resting, we don't want to go barging in."

As he spoke, he tapped on the door. Diana grabbed his arm and pulled him back behind the staircase. "We cannot be seen, Ronald," she warned. They listened, but no one came to the door.

Diana realized by this time that her helper was incompetent, and she tried to pry open the lock with a hairpin and later a nail file. When neither worked, she suggested they go outside and try to get in by a window. Ronald promptly walked to the largest window facing the street and began hauling it.

"The back window, Ron," she said, pointing to a few people on the street who had already stopped to stare at them. They slipped through a narrow alley and found themselves in a small, dark yard with pale windows gleaming in the moonlight.

"I can't reach them," Ronald said. "There's no way in, Di. We might as well go home!"

"The letters that will save Harrup's reputation and secure you a good future are in those empty rooms. Are you going to let a quarter of an inch of glass stop you?" she demanded.

"It's not the glass. It's the height."

Diana looked all around the yard. "What's that dark lump over there?" she asked.

Ronald walked toward it and said, "A rain barrel, but I can't move it. It's full."

"We shall empty it," his sister informed him through thin lips, and strode purposefully toward it.

"Damme, you've got water all over my shoes," Ronald complained as the sluggish water splashed to the ground.

"Never mind your shoes. I've destroyed my second-best gown and probably my good cape as well. I'm going to take it off." She tossed her sable-trimmed cape aside and helped her brother roll the barrel to the window. "I'll steady it while you climb up," she said.

Ronald, with many slips and tumbles, was finally at the proper height. "The window's locked inside," he said. There was a noticeable accent of relief in his voice.

"I'll find a rock," Diana replied promptly, and scrabbled around at the edge of the garden till she had one so heavy she could hardly lift it. Her gloves, she knew, were a shambles, and her coiffure had long since lost its style. "Break it softly," she advised.

Ronald tapped gently at the pane. "Harder than that," she said, becoming impatient with him.

Ronald swung his arm back and heaved. The ear-splitting noise was by no means the worst of it. Slivers of glass flew in all directions. Ronald howled and fell to the ground, clutching his eyes.

"Oh, my God!" Diana rushed forward. "Are you all right? Ronald, you didn't cut your eyes?"

His hands came down slowly. He blinked and sat up. "I can see," he breathed. Then he glanced at his fingers, where a dab of blood was visible in the moonlight. "I'm wounded," he moaned, and lay down on the cold, damp ground. "Steeped in my own blood."

"Where are you hurt?" A close examination showed a cut a quarter of an inch long on one finger. "Why didn't you wear your gloves?" she asked.

"I didn't want to destroy them."

Diana's attention was divided between her brother and the house. A head came to the window on the lower right-side apartment. She held Ronald still, hoping the shadows would conceal them. In a moment, the head receded and all was quiet. "I didn't mean break it that hard," she said, fear turning to anger now that the danger had past.

"Well, if that ain't—just how hard should I have broken it? Tell me that."

"You should have protected your face, at least. Never mind, we must get inside while we have the chance. That would be the kitchen window you broke, I think. You go in first and give me a hand."

"Can you staunch this wound first?" he asked ironically, when another drop of blood oozed from his finger.

"I can't even find it."

Ronald returned to the barrel, where he leisurely pulled shards of glass from the frame to permit himself to enter unscathed. Diana waited below, fuming impotently. At last the entry was deemed safe, and Ronald crawled in head-first, his legs sticking out the window and wiggling till finally they disappeared and his head popped out.

"It's the pantry," he whispered.

Diana was already balanced on the barrel. Ronald's help proved so bothersome that she finally told him to stand back while she hoisted herself up to the window ledge and squirmed her way in. Soon they stood together in a small pantry, listening to make sure they were alone. When all remained quiet beyond, they ventured forth into the dining room and on to the saloon.

"There must be a study," Diana said, looking around in the shadowed room.

"What we need is a light," Ronald decided, and began knocking over tables and chairs till he found a flint box. After much fumbling, the lamp was lit. Diana cautioned him to dim the flame by holding a paper in front of it, and they went forward looking for Markwell's office.

"Here it is," Ronald said, and darted in, straight to the bookshelves. "What a paltry collection," he scoffed. "No Virgil, no Cicero, not even Homer. I could forgive the rest, for Homer is all a man truly needs. Imagine an illiterate like that being a member of Parliament! All his books are in English."

Diana decided the bookshelf was as good a place as any to keep Ronald out of mischief. She closed the door, took the lamp, and headed straight to the desk. The top drawer was locked, the others unlocked. She quickly rifled the open ones, knowing in her heart that if the letters were there, they would be under lock and key. "We've got to break into this drawer," she told her brother.

Over his shoulder Ronald said, "Yes, go ahead, Di. I'm just looking at this copy of *Waverley*. I haven't read Scott, but the chaps say he's very good. I wonder if Markwell would mind if I borrowed it."

With a resigned shake of her head, Diana reached for a brass letter opener and pried the lock till she had broken it. The drawer slid open, and at the back she spotted a corner of pink satin ribbon. She reached in and pulled out the familiar billets-doux.

"I found them!" she exclaimed triumphantly, and stuffed them into her reticule. "Let's go before someone comes."

"Listen to this, Di," Ronald said, smiling. " 'A sneaking piece of imbecility' Scott calls Edward Waverley. This does sound good."

"Put the book back and let us go," she said.

"I only meant to borrow it."

A sound of movement behind the closed door was heard at the same instant by them both. They exchanged frightened, wide-eyed stares and looked to the door. The handle turned slowly. Diana had awful visions of Lord Markwell, pistol in hand. Her mind went perfectly blank, but just before the door opened, she recovered sufficiently at least to blow out the lamp and plunge them into darkness. Instinct led her to crouch behind the desk for concealment.

When the door opened silently, the first thing she saw around the desk's corner was another lit lamp. Hovering above it was a man's ugly, common face. Only a servant, she thought with some relief. The man spotted Ronald near the door in an instant. He raised his lamp and gave a gloating smile.

"Caught you snaffling the goods, eh, mate? A rum gent like you, all done up in style. What would you be doing a thing like that for?"

"I was only borrowing it!" Ronald said, offense in every line of his slender body.

"Sure you was, and didn't plan to help yourself to his lordship's jewels and silver, either. Oh, no, not a fine dandy like you. You can tell it to the watch house preacher, lad."

Realizing that the servant thought Ronald was alone, Diana held her breath and prayed her brother wouldn't tell the man she was there. Though he wouldn't purposely hurt a fly, it would be just like him to blurt it out. She began looking around for a weapon to knock the servant out and free Ronald. At least the man didn't carry a gun.

Before she could find anything, the man took Ronald by the arm and hauled him from the study, thinking he'd caught an ordinary criminal, come to loot the flat. She listened, heart pounding, as Ronald protested his innocence. "An outrage! I just came to borrow a book."

"And decided to let yourself in by smashing the glass.

59

Lucky chance for me I was only next door having a heavy wet with a buddy and heard you. Come along easy, lad. It'd be a shame to have to darken your pretty daylights and draw your cork.''

These menacing words turned Ronald completely docile. He allowed himself to be taken away, and Diana found herself alone and shaking like a leaf in Lord Markwell's study. As the flat was now empty, she left by the front door and ran around the corner to Harrup's carriage, to follow Ronald to whatever watch house he was taken to. When she saw him being led in, she pulled the check string and spoke to Harrup's groom.

"Would it be proper for a young lady to go in and bail him out?'' she asked calmly.

"No, miss. It wouldn't. What you'd best do is tell his lordship what happened.''

"Oh, I don't think it's a very good idea to bother his lordship,'' she said, biting her underlip. "Perhaps *you* would be kind enough?'' she suggested, glancing to the watch house.

"You need bail money, you see, miss, which I don't have. 'Sides beyond, they'd not put him under the protection of such a one as myself. It's his lordship you must tell.''

"Very well,'' she agreed, and settled back against the squabs, clutching the precious letters. Harrup couldn't cut up very stiff when she had recovered his letters. She ardently hoped the Grodens were not making a night of it at the house.

John Groom apparently deemed the errand urgent, for he bolted the carriage in great haste to Belgrave Square, while Diana was jostled around inside. She went around to the kitchen door to discover who was in the house.

"Good Lord above us,'' Miss Peabody shrieked when she saw her bedraggled charge, her hair tumbling about her ears; her gown was soiled and ripped at the waist from

60

squirming in the window, and the hem of her dress covered in mud. "What happened to you?"

"We had an accident," Diana said briefly. "Ronald is—is just fine. I left him off at his rooms. Is Harrup here, and have the Grodens left?"

"They just went out the door a minute ago. Diana, you must not let Harrup see you like that. Where is your cape? Was it stolen?"

"My cape!" she exclaimed. "Oh, dear!" It was not fear of being identified by the garment that bothered her, but its loss. It was her very best, especially beloved for its sable collar. "I'll have to go back for it."

"Back where? Where did it happen?"

"It's rather urgent, Peabody. I'll see Harrup first, then tell you."

"He's in his study," Mrs. Dunaway told her.

"Thank you, Mrs. Dunaway," Diana said very formally, and scampered upstairs, her muddied hem dragging behind her.

Harrup had just sat at his desk and poured himself a glass of wine. He was weary from an evening with his in-laws-to-be. Groden was a dead bore, his lady a mute, and with the parents along, there had been no privacy with Selena. In fact, the girl hardly glanced at him. A shy little thing, but beautiful. His eyes glazed over as he remembered her raven curls and ivory skin, her pellucid blue eyes and those cherry lips. She was very well built for a young girl, too. He looked up impatiently when the tap came at the door.

"Come in."

The door opened slowly, and a bedraggled person he hardly recognized smiled at him. He soon recognized that bold pixie smile and the slanting eyes full of mischief. "Missie! What the devil—"

"I got them, Harrup! I got your letters." She beamed and hopped forward to lay them on his desk.

"You got the letters? How?" He stared from woman to letters in bewilderment.

"I'll tell you all about it on the way to the watch house," she said, shooting a nervous glance at him.

Harrup's eyes widened in dismay. "The—what?"

"Unfortunately Ronald got caught, but they think he was only stealing Walter Scott."

A great feeling of foreboding came over Harrup. He glared and pointed with one finger at a chair by his desk. "Sit!" he commanded.

Diana sank gratefully onto the chair. "I am rather tired," she admitted. "It was quite fatiguing moving the barrel and getting in the window. It was a tight fit, but I could not let Ronald smash the front window, because of the people on the street." She spotted the wine and poured herself a glass, which she gulped, then sighed wearily.

"Am I to understand you and that cawker of a brother broke into Lord Markwell's flat and stole the letters?" he asked. His voice sounded hollow, as though he were shouting down a long corridor. *"And got caught?"* he added.

"Only Ronald. I got away with the letters." She pointed to the stack on his desk. "It wasn't Markwell himself who caught us. It was only a servant. Oh, I do hope Ronald has the wits to give a false name at the watch house. Do you think he will, Harrup?"

"No. A boy who doesn't know enough to wipe behind the ears will hardly be on to it. Where is he?"

"I'll have to show you. I followed him in your carriage, but I couldn't tell you the address. I was discreet! We stayed well behind them. No one will suspect you are involved."

"My going to bail Ronald out will slip them the clue. The fact that you're staying at my house is confirmation, not that it's needed."

Diana pondered this a moment. "That's true. You'll have

62

to give a false name, too—or you could have someone else do it for you."

"Lord Eldon, perhaps?" he suggested satirically. "The lord chancellor should have no difficulty gaining Ronald's freedom. Or would you prefer I ask my future father-in-law, Lord Groden, the stiffest rump in England, to do it?"

Diana looked at the letters, carelessly tossed on his desk, and felt she was being treated shabbily. "It's the least you could do! We did it all for you, and it was neither easy nor pleasant, I assure you. Look at my dress—ruined. My best slippers have turned to mush," she added, lifting a foot to show him. "To say nothing of my sable-trimmed cape," she added, for this was considered the greatest loss.

Harrup cast a sympathetic eye at the well-turned ankle and sighed wearily. "Thank you, Diana. I am happy to have the letters back. You've done more than enough tonight. Go upstairs and have a bath, and I'll bail Ronald out."

"I have to go with you," she said simply.

"Housebreaking and stealing weren't sufficient amusement for one night? You want to top it off with a visit to a watch house?"

"Yes, I do," she agreed. "I've never seen one before. But I expect I'll have to wait in the carriage. I want to talk to Ronald and make sure he's all right. He got wounded in the—"

Harrup jerked to attention. "Not shot!"

"Oh, no. Just cut a little when he smashed the window. The idiot took off his gloves. I told him not to hit it so hard. At least Markwell's servant was not at all violent."

A trip to the watch house seemed tame after Diana's other activities, and as Harrup was eager both to free Ronald and hear the story, he agreed to let her come along.

"You'd best lock those letters up before we go," she suggested.

"We know how efficacious a lock is," he answered, and

tucked them in his inside pocket. He placed his own evening cape over Diana's shoulders and called his carriage. While they rattled along to free Ronald, she gave him a lively account of their evening activities.

"I found myself wishing you were there, Harrup," she admitted.

"Thank you. So do not I!"

"You would have scolded like a fishwife, but you would have known how to handle the servant. Ronald is a very indifferent accomplice. If he hadn't started reading Walter Scott and fallen into a passion, we would have been home free. Which is not to say that he's incompetent in other areas," she added hastily when she recalled her ultimate aim. "He is very bookish and intelligent. He was shocked at the gaps in Markwell's library. Ronald will make someone an excellent secretary."

With an ironic lift of his brow, Harrup said, "Perhaps Mr. Scott could use him."

This was obviously not the most auspicious moment to dun Harrup for a position. Diana decided that must wait till he had enjoyed a good night's sleep, easy that his letters were safe and, she hoped, forgetful of having had to rescue the rescuer. She remained in the carriage till Harrup had bailed Ronald out.

"Where do you live?" he asked Ronald when the dejected young gentleman was safe in the carriage.

Ronald gave him the address, and with very little conversation, for the Beechams could see that Harrup was in the boughs, the carriage took Mr. Beecham home.

"Naturally, I shall reimburse you tomorrow," Ronald said stiffly when he alighted from the rig.

"Just be sure you present yourself at Bow Street at ten tomorrow morning. I hope Markwell sends his servant, and doesn't take into his head to go himself," Harrup growled.

Diana cleared her throat and said softly, "It would be a good idea if you declare a meeting for nine-thirty tomorrow morning, Harrup, to ensure that Markwell is at Westminster at ten.''

He glowered and said, "You've taken over my private life. Pray restrain yourself from entering politics.''

Diana cleared her throat again nervously and said, "Yes, indeed, but before we go home, would you mind taking us back to Lord Markwell's house? I must pick up my cape,'' she explained to her companion.

"You left your cape there?'' Harrup asked, staring. "No doubt your reticule was left behind as well, with your calling cards in it.''

"Certainly not! I held on to it very carefully as it contained your love notes to Mrs. Whitby. And my cape is not in Markwell's flat. It is in his backyard, if someone hasn't stolen it.''

"Where is Markwell's place?''

She directed him to Glasshouse Street.

"This is why you were pestering me for Markwell's address,'' he accused.

"I told you what I meant to do.''

"And I told you not to do it!''

"But I got your billets-doux back,'' she pointed out.

There was no arguing with that, and Harrup was so relieved that he directed the carriage to Glasshouse Street with no further ado.

Chapter Five

"There, that's the place," Diana said as Harrup's carriage approached Markwell's house. "If you'll have the groom stop, I'll just pop out and pick up my cape. I know exactly where I left it."

Harrup gave a grudging smile. "This evening goes from melodrama to farce. No, Diana, you will not just pop out and fall into some other scrape. Tell me where you mislaid the cursed cape and I'll get it."

"It is not mislaid. I placed it very carefully aside to keep it from getting wet—wetter. It's somewhere behind the barrel, which is at the window. And Harrup, do be careful. The servant might just possibly be peeking out the window. I wouldn't want to involve you in anything unsavory," she said.

He mistrusted the pixie tilt of her eyes and some quality in her voice that was just short of a gurgle. "You enjoy putting me through my paces," he accused.

"It will do you no harm to be knocked off your high horse from time to time. A man must expect to pay for his sins."

Harrup tried to go on acting angry, but his innate sense of the ridiculous took over when he found the sodden cape on the ground and imagined the sequence of events that had led to it. He rather wished he had been there.

"Open the windows," he ordered as he got in. "This thing smells like a wet rat."

"Oh, my poor sable!" Diana said, stroking it. "I shan't be able to lord it over the other ladies at the local assemblies without my sable-collared cape. I hope Peabody will be able to resuscitate it."

"Peabody could resuscitate a mummy. May we go home now? It's only eleven. We have time to rob a bank or beat up the watch."

"Not this evening, thank you. Home will be fine."

"I take it you didn't get around to seeing the play at Drury Lane?" he asked.

"No, but Ronald can take me tomorrow evening."

"Tell him not to purchase tickets. I have a box. I'm taking Selena—we'll all go together."

"It is not at all necessary to feel you have to reward us. We were very happy to give a helping hand. What are friends for?"

"No further propaganda will be necessary before you dun me for your favor, Diana. I wish you would tell me what it is you're going to make me do. I'm becoming nervous at the delay."

"I shall be asking very soon, but meanwhile please don't bother with *small* favors. Ronald can take me to Drury Lane," Diana told him.

"I'm not doing a favor. I'm asking one from you in this matter," he explained. "My hope is to prevent the Grodens from filling the extra seats in my box. After an evening in their company, I am merely ensuring my own sanity. The man's conversation is the greatest bore since Milton penned *Paradise Lost*."

"Oh, do you hate it, too?" Diana asked, and laughed. "I never could see what all the excitement was about. In that case, we shall be very happy to do you *another* favor, Harrup."

When they returned, Diana followed Harrup into his office. He looked at her questioningly. "The letters," she said. "I want to make sure they're all there, safe and sound."

Harrup pulled them from his pocket and removed the pink ribbon. He flipped through the stack quickly, then cast a frowning look at Diana. "There are two missing."

"No! I counted them. The six were there. Look again."

"Six? I wrote Laura eight letters."

They regarded each other in consternation. "She only gave me six," Diana assured him. "I'm positive. Peabody and I counted them twice."

Harrup began pulling out the sheets and scanning them. He cast each aside on the desk as he finished. Diana picked them up and glanced at them. As he didn't object, she began to read one through. Her cheeks turned pink and she stared at Harrup in astonishment.

He was busy and didn't notice her expression. "She kept the warmest ones," Harrup said, and emitted a proficient curse. "First, she leads Markwell to this lot to let him steal my appointment, then she keeps the worst of the bunch to hold me to ransom and make me a laughingstock. I can't believe Laura would act so badly. I'll be ruined if she takes into her head to publish them—or shows them to Groden! My God!"

Diana blinked at him. "Warmer than this?" she asked, looking at the letter. " 'Every hour away from your alabaster arms seems a day, every day an eternity. . . .' "

Harrup, blushing furiously, took it from her and crushed it into a ball. She promptly took up another. " 'Eyes like star sapphires set in alabaster marble,' " she read, and giggled. "More alabaster. The woman sounds like a quarry. Such lack of originality! I thought you would make love more convincingly."

Harrup snatched the lot and threw them into the fireplace. One sheet came loose, and Diana ran after it. He grabbed her wrist and spun her around. Laughing, Diana held the letter behind her back, beyond his reach. "No, do let me see what other marble features Mrs. Whitby possesses."

Harrup reached behind her back with his other hand till she was encircled in his arms. As he bent over her, he found himself gazing into her laughing eyes. Tendrils of golden curls framed her forehead and tumbled forward over her cheeks, which were pink and soft and not at all like marble. Her lips were open, revealing a straight row of pearly teeth. Warm breaths fanned his cheek.

"Say please, Harrup," she teased, and danced away.

Harrup let her go, but stood looking at her with a peculiar, conscious expression in his eyes. For a flashing instant he had felt a strong urge to pull her into his arms and kiss her. Even now he was aware of how well she filled that striped gown, how slender her waist and how full her breasts, how attractive she looked despite her disarray. It was the liveliness that did it. Di was always a lively girl. She had blossomed into a very alluring woman, but still kept that youthful sense of fun and adventure.

He felt uneasy with these thoughts and thought she was uneasy, too. When he took a step toward her, she handed him the letter with a shy smile. "I was only fooling," she said, and went immediately to sit primly at his desk. "What are you going to do about Mrs. Whitby, Harrup?"

"Pay her," he said grimly. "I don't have many options. I wonder she hasn't sent me a menacing note before now."

"I wouldn't give her a sou if I were you."

"If you knew how much I want that appointment, you would. And with my marriage to Selena approaching—it would be a wretched embarrassment to the poor girl. Groden's kept her bundled in cotton wool. She has no notion what I—what men—that is . . ."

"How old is she?"

"Eighteen, I think."

"Eighteen!" Diana exclaimed, staring in disbelief.

69

"You're marrying a child of eighteen! Good God, you're twice her age. How can you—" She noticed the stiffening of Harrup's jaw and fell silent, though her rebukeful gaze lingered.

"It is not at all unusual for a man of my years to marry a lady making her debut."

"Yes, I suppose so," Diana agreed. "But it seems wrong, somehow. So you plan to pay Whitby—five thousand, I think you mentioned."

"Not a penny less. She has a pretty accurate idea what I'm worth and what she might reasonably try to squeeze out of me."

Diana blinked. "Five thousand," she said pensively. "That is every penny I'm worth in the world. Imagine, a couple of sheets of your scribbling are worth my entire dot."

Harrup shrugged indifferently. "To put it another way, your dot is worth the attorney generalship, if that makes you feel more valuable."

"But still, it is too much to give to a scoundrel like Mrs. Whitby. We *must* get the letters back."

"No!" Harrup stated very firmly. "*We* shall do nothing of the sort. I have always treated Laura well, however, and I shall make a visit to try to charm them out of her."

She gave him a quelling look. "You'll end up writing her another batch of drivel that will turn up when you're trying to become lord chancellor. No, Harrup, object though you may—and shall—I am the one who must get your letters. Now let me see," she said, and frowned into the distance. "It's a pity she's met me, or I might try to scrape an acquaintance under some alias and weasel my way into her confidence."

"You would pose as a member of the muslin company, I expect?" Harrup asked, lips unsteady.

"Why, no, merely a maker of bonnets or gowns for such boudoir aristocracy. Naturally, I do not suggest this raddled old countenance would ever incite a gent to fork over his blunt—or compromise his judgment by running off at the pen. I leave that to alabaster ladies with eyes like star sapphires and hearts of forged steel,'' she finished, trying to stare him down.

Harrup regarded her for a moment, and when he spoke, he seemed to have forgotten their discussion. ''How old are you now, Di?''

''A hundred and twenty-five, give or take a century. Why do you ask?''

''You should have been on the market a few years ago when you were—'' Harrup stopped, aware by the glitter in her eyes that he was giving offense.

''What, are there no *partis* twice my age on the town? Surely there must be a few doddering widowers on the catch for such a well-aged article as I.''

''I have trod on your toes. Sorry, my dear. I didn't mean to imply you were over the hill.''

Diana dismissed the apology with such casual indifference that Harrup knew she was untouched. ''This tough old hide doesn't wound easily. To return to business, Mrs. Whitby said she would be seeing you in London soon. Can you discover whether she has arrived?''

''I expect I shall be the first to know,'' he replied through thin lips.

She shook her head. ''No, Markwell will be the first to know. They're obviously working together. He followed us to the inn in Hitchin and stole your letters. He could only have known our route if she told him. He was with her when he told you he was visiting his father. He must be her new lover. Why else would she share her letters with him? She wants to give her lover a leg up the ladder and saw a means of embarrassing you into the bargain. Hell hath no fury like a woman scorned,'' she added sagely.

Harrup considered this, but he was far from convinced. ''Why would she bother giving you any letters at all? She could have told me she burned them, and given them all to Markwell.''

"I don't know," Diana admitted. "That is odd, now you mention it. Unless—I don't know. Perhaps she only wanted to embarrass you without showing her own hand. But in that case she would have given Markwell *all* the letters."

"I still can't believe Laura would do such a thing. I go along with you to the point where Markwell was with her and she told him she was giving you my letters, but I don't believe she encouraged him to steal them. That was his own idea."

"Why did she keep the warmest ones?" Diana asked.

Harrup's frown softened to a smile. "For sentimental reasons. We're looking for trouble where there is none. Laura has no intention of trying to get money from me for the letters."

Diana just shook her head. "You actually believe she has them wrapped in lavender, to read when she's feeling lonesome? How can a fully grown man be such an idiot?" she asked in a purely rhetorical spirit.

"How can you be so cynical? Damsels are supposed to be idealistic, romantically inclined."

"It is only attractive gentlemen we idealize. She had a sly smile, Harrup. You haven't heard the end of this."

"I'll make some inquiries and discover if Laura has come to town yet. If she has, I'll call on her and turn her up sweet."

Diana rose and yawned. "Take your checkbook with you," she suggested. "It always works with Peabody. And now I am off to bed."

She took up her muddied cape and left the room. Harrup remained behind, thinking. He thought he had the matter figured out. Laura had taken Markwell for her new lover; he had been with her and pirated the letters from Peabody, but those letters were now safe, and Laura—dear Laura—

had no intention of using the other two letters to embarrass him. Still, he'd take along a small piece of jewelry when he visited her. A brooch or a bracelet—or cash might be more convenient. Markwell wasn't well to grass. Best to keep Laura in good spirits.

The next morning, Peabody learned from Diana that the letters had been recovered, though she wasn't quite clear how this miracle had happened. "Found them where, Di? They were not lying in the street."

"You'd have to ask Ronald. I believe he called on Markwell and came across them in the man's study."

"But where were you during all this? Don't tell me Ronald took you to call on a bachelor!"

"No, no. I waited in the carriage."

"How did your cape get destroyed sitting in a carriage?"

"I dropped it—accidentally."

"Wouldn't you know it would land in a puddle," Peabody said, well able to believe it of fate.

The important thing was that the letters were secure, and Peabody felt brave enough to take breakfast with Harrup and Diana. Di got Harrup aside and informed him of the vague manner in which his letters had been recovered.

"What frivolities do you ladies have in mind for the day?" he asked.

"We might as well head back home," Peabody answered. "We have your letters safely back and Ronald settled in. I dread to think of him living in those cramped quarters, poor boy. Isn't it a caution how he knew Markwell and could drop in to see him? I never thought he would be so clever." Di glared hard. "Of course, he is up to all the rigs—a regular dasher."

Diana hurried in to change the subject. "Harrup has invited Ronald and me to Drury Lane this evening." Peabody glowed, taking it as a compliment to herself.

Diana figured that she would ask Harrup about a job for

Ronald that evening, when Lady Selena had him in a good mood. "We can go home tomorrow," she said to her chaperon.

"Why don't you stay a few days?" Harrup suggested.

Peabody cast a benign eye on her Chuggie and said, "We don't want to impose on your hospitality."

"Impose?" he asked, and laughed. "I imposed on your good nature for several years, Peabody. I have an empty house at the moment. I hope you will consider it your home. Stay a week. Di's in no rush to get back to the Willows, are you?" he finished, turning to her.

"No, there's nothing to go home to," she admitted.

He shook his head in sympathy. "As bad as that, is it? You really ought to submit your name at court and make a debut. Some doddering old bachelor would have you," he joked.

Peabody laughed inanely to show Diana how she was to receive this compliment. "Chuggie was always a prime jokesmith," she said.

"I'm sure his wit is much appreciated in the House, if it can be heard above the snores."

Peabody soon left to begin work on the soiled cape, which had to be ready for Drury Lane that evening, and Diana went with Harrup while he got his hat and gloves. "I hope everything goes all right with Ronald at Bow Street this morning," she said.

"Don't worry your head about that. Markwell's servant will produce the *Waverley* novel as evidence, Ron will pay his fine, and that will be an end to it."

"Yes, but Markwell will know by now that the letters were stolen, and—"

"What can he do about it?" Harrup asked with satisfaction. "He can hardly report them as stolen. He won't show his nose at Bow Street. Don't worry. But I'll keep a sharp eye on him, see how he acts toward me. I'm off now. Enjoy your day, Diana."

74

He gave her fingers a light squeeze and left. The sun shone brightly as he stepped out to his curricle. He had his letters back, and soon he would receive notice of his appointment. It had been enjoyable to have some female company at breakfast. Before long he would have the daily pleasure of Selena's pretty face across from him. Selena was not quite so lively as Diana, of course, but when she became more at home with him, she'd open like a rosebud in the sun. She was still a child really, eighteen. Approximately half his age. When he was fifty, she'd be thirty-three. In her prime, while he was on the down road. Foolish to worry about that so soon. Selena wasn't the sort of lady to cause her husband worries. A nice, docile child—*lady*!

Diana's day was busy. Ronald came directly to her from Bow Street. He had escaped with a fine of three guineas— a blow, but not crushing. Markwell had not been there, and best of all, he had had the wits to use an alias. Whether George Cuthbert would be happy that his name was the one that popped into Ronald's head was a matter of some concern, but as he had no intention of telling Cuthbert, he soon forgot that detail.

"I daresay Harrup was very grateful we got his letters back for him, once he settled down," he said, looking hopefully to hear what form the gratitude had taken.

"I didn't ask him about the position for you yet, Ronald. Tonight we shall do it, after we come home from the theater. As it turns out, two of the letters are still missing. Harrup is not worried, but I am. I feel in my bones Mrs. Whitby means to make mischief with them. If we can save Harrup five thousand guineas, he cannot reasonably offer you anything less than the post as his assistant."

As Ronald was still at leisure, they spent the afternoon touring London. Diana purchased new gloves at the Pantheon Bazaar. Hers had been totally destroyed the night before. To make up for dragging her brother through the bazaar, Diana dallied at bookstalls with Ronald while he searched for a copy of *Waverley*. Once the two volumes were in his hands, it was hard to interest him in anything else. Diana directed the groom to drive them through all the parks. She spared not a glance for the newly leafed trees, the sun glowing through their branches and dappling the grass below. She could see that at home. Her interest was riveted on the fine gentlemen and ladies, their equipages sparkling, their matched teams groomed to perfection. Ronald stuck his nose into a book and read.

They had tea at a country inn, Ronald still reading, which caused rather more spilling than usual, while Diana looked around at the other customers. She took the liberty of inviting Ronald to dine at Harrup's, but with his nose firmly implanted in the book, he refused. She thought the word he muttered was "Cuthbert" and assumed Ronald was dining with this friend. Just before she left him at his flat, he said, "I have been seduced, Di. I never thought I would burn out my eyes on mere novels, but this is really something out of the ordinary. I think you must make my apologies to Harrup this evening. I shall stay home and finish this book."

"You will do nothing of the sort! You are my escort, and you will be at Belgrave Square at seven-thirty."

"Then I'd best hurry in. I can be done with this first volume by seven, and read the second tonight. Oh, damme, there is Cuthbert pacing the street, waiting for me. I'll get rid of him."

Diana drove home and made her toilette for the evening. As her embroidered cape was a little spotted, she decided the elegance of her blue satin was required to compensate. At least she would look unexceptionable once she removed the cape. Harrup's dark eyes made an appreciative tour of her toilette, admiring the white shoulders against the blue gown and thinking to himself that alabaster was the only word for them, but he dared not say it. "That should bring the octogenarians out of the woodwork'' was his offhand compliment.

"I wish you would quit staring at me as if I were beef-steak," she complained, though she was actually surprised to see that glint of masculine admiration in his eyes, and not displeased, either.

"Beefsteak is the wrong metaphor. You look more like dessert—delectably sweet."

"Stick to alabaster, Harrup," she advised, and twitched away.

Peabody joined them for dinner, and the compliments ceased. In a nostalgic mood, she regaled them with apocryphal tales of Harrup's precocity in the nursery.

"He knew where everything was kept," she told Diana, shaking her head in wonder. "No one could believe it. I remember one day I was ill—the earache always plagued me—and Bessie McGill, who was replacing me, couldn't credit her eyes. 'Where does Peabody keep the nappies?' she asked, just talking aloud to herself, you know, and what should Chuggie do but crawl straight to the cupboard and open the door. There were the nappies. It was no accident, for it was the same with everything she asked for. At nine months he recognized every word and knew where all his things were stored."

"Are you quite sure he crawled to the cupboard, Peabody?" Diana quizzed. "I'm sure you told me Chuggie was walking at nine months."

"Not when he was in a hurry. He *could* walk at nine months, but he had the cutest way of dragging himself across the floor, pulling one foot behind him when he was in a hurry. My, what a mess he made of his frocks."

Diana turned a mocking gaze on Harrup. "He sounds adorable. Remarkable how he has changed."

"She is only funning," Peabody assured Harrup. "You never knew such a lively soul, Chuggie. How she makes fun of all the beaux at the assemblies at home. She can mimic the vicar's droll tones to a T. Do the vicar for Chuggie, Di.''

Harrup turned a laughing eye on her. ''Turnabout is fair play, milady. Your turn.''

''You show me the famous dragging crawl and I'll do the vicar,'' Diana bargained.

When the meal was finished, Peabody informed Harrup she was going to her room to knit him a new pair of slippers, for she was sure those shoes must be uncomfortable after a hard day at work. ''Now that you are about to settle into a married man,'' she said coyly, ''your days of running around town are numbered. You will want to spend the evenings with your lady by the fireside. I'm sure she has all accomplishments, Harrup. You were always so demanding in that regard—remember how you used to scold about your mama's friends. 'No conversation,' you used to say, though I'm sure the talk never flagged a moment. It will be quite like old times, having the nursery occupied again.'' She sighed happily.

''Thank you, Peabody. You are too kind,'' Harrup said, concealing his impatience as best he could.

Peabody gushed happily and went to search out her woolens. Not till she had left did Harrup turn a leary eye on Diana. ''My God, how long have you had to listen to tales of my ingenuity?''

''For twenty-five years.'' She sighed. ''You may imagine our astonishment when such a paragon as dear Chuggie turned out to have feet of clay.''

''Peabody was sadly disillusioned with me over the Whitby affair, I should think?'' he asked.

''You underestimate the height of your pedestal. It is all Mrs. Whitby's fault. She preys on innocent young thirty-five-year-olds. Reality and Peabody's memories run in separate channels. By the way, it was kind of you to go and visit her downstairs yesterday. I forgot to thank you.''

"It is I who should thank you for drawing it to my attention. I should have thought of it myself."

"You're very busy," Diana said forgivingly. "Dear me, I'm beginning to sound like Peabody!" She smiled. "Let us go. Lady Selena may not be so understanding if we're late."

They left to call for Lady Selena. Harrup asked Diana to go into the Grodens' house with him, but she elected to wait in the carriage. It was there that she had her first view of Lady Selena. Even in the dim light she could see the girl was an incomparable. A wave of black hair swept from her high forehead. The color of her eyes was indistinguishable, but their large size and luminosity were apparent, as were the contours of her face. A high cheek, a small nose, the face tapering to a nearly perfect heart shape below. Yet with all this beauty and high birth, there was no sign of haughtiness in the girl. Diana waited to hear how the vision spoke. The soft, hesitant voice was childish.

"I am pleased to make your acquaintance, Miss Beecham," she said, and for the remainder of the trip she said virtually nothing.

Harrup prodded her to speech by making leading statements. "Miss Beecham is my neighbor at home," he said.

Lady Selena smiled shyly.

"I hope we shall see a good deal of each other after you are married," Diana said to fill the silence.

A faint "Yes" was whispered in the darkness.

"Do you ride? There are some lovely rides at Harrup Hall," Diana said. Her voice sounded loud and harsh to her own ears.

"A little. Not much," Lady Selena replied. Her tone was apologetic.

Harrup clapped his hands and tried another tack. "So we are off to Drury Lane. I always enjoy Sheridan. Such a wit the man has."

"Do you like Sheridan, Lady Selena?" Diana asked.

"I—I don't think I have seen him act before," Lady Selena replied.

"Sheridan is the playwright, Selena, not the actor," Harrup told her.

"Oh."

"*The School for Scandal* is one of his best. I'm sure you'll enjoy it," Diana said.

Another quiet yes hung on the air.

Harrup, not a patient man, gave up and turned his talk to Diana. "We should have asked Peabody to join us. Why didn't you remind me?"

"Peabody doesn't like going out. The fates can find her better at home."

"She is still the target for all malign forces, is she?" he asked, smiling.

"Certainly. The day before we left home the postman purposely ripped the cover from her favorite periodical. It was only my vigilance that kept Jennie from destroying her blue muslin with bleach." Diana turned to try to include Lady Selena in the conversation. "Peabody was Harrup's nursemaid and mine. She is now my chaperon," she explained.

Lady Selena smiled and nodded.

"You might as well learn her oddities," Diana added. "Very likely she will end up running your nursery."

Lady Selena squirmed uncomfortably. She didn't honor this effort with a smile. Diana thought perhaps her remark was in bad taste and quickly changed the topic. "Do you have any brothers and sisters?" she asked.

"Yes."

"Selena has two brothers and three sisters," Harrup added, and filled the next few blocks with an enumeration of them and their positions.

"I have just one brother, Ronald," Diana said, and took her turn at talking till the carriage reached Drury Lane. "Oh, there is Ronald now, waiting for us," she exclaimed.

80

Selena glanced out the window with moderate interest. She was surprised Miss Beecham should have such a nice-looking brother. She was afraid he would be big and old and brusque like Harrup, but he looked very sensitive and not of an overwhelming size. They alighted and Harrup made the introductions. Lady Selena cranked her courage up to curtsy and say, "I am pleased to meet you, Mr. Beecham."

Diana waited on thorns for Ronald to trip or step on Lady Selena's gown or knock her evening bag from her hand. He did none of these things as he stood motionless as a stone, staring at the vision of loveliness before him. The only little embarrassment was that he fell utterly speechless. He stared, with his lower lip fallen, and didn't say a word. He had never seen or imagined such exquisite perfection existed in the real world. She was the embodiment of Mr. Scott's heroine, the gentle Rose Bradwardine.

Diana took his arm, Harrup placed his hand on Lady Selena's elbow, and the four entered the theater. Harrup had a box on the grand tier. Diana was so thrilled with the glamour of the occasion that she forgot Lady Selena. She looked around at the crowd of bejeweled ladies and elegant gentlemen and smiled happily. How wonderful it was to be in London, rubbing elbows with the tip of the ton.

"You must be very successful, Ronald," she said. "I want you to hire a grand house and let me be your hostess. Wouldn't it be wonderful to live here?"

"Did you mention the position to Harrup?" Ronald asked in a low voice.

"Not yet. He's still much worried about the missing letters."

"That's odd," he said. "Cuthbert made me go out to dinner with him this evening. I hardly got a chapter read, for he chattered like a magpie all through dinner. He got an increase in his allowance from his papa and hired one of the top floor flats on Glasshouse Street—Markwell's place, you know. I told you he had been looking at it. The strange thing is, he told me a very beautiful lady had just taken the other flat. A lady of a certain age with black hair. He didn't mention her name, but I wonder if she could be Mrs. Whitby.''

"I'll wager she is," Diana said, her heart racing in excitement. "Markwell would let her know the flat was for hire, and they would want to be close together, yet maintain a semblance of respectability.'' She wanted to inform Harrup and looked to the front of the stall to see if he was engaged in conversation.

She saw him staring off at the crowd, completely neglectful of his companion, who stared the other way, equally bored. She looked from one profile to the other. Harrup's jaw was clamped, giving him an angry look. Lady Selena appeared all of ten or twelve—a veritable child, though undeniably beautiful.

Following his sister's gaze, Ronald said, "Isn't she exquisite?''

"Talk to her, Ronald. I want to speak to Harrup."

Ronald leaned forward and said in his gentle voice that couldn't frighten a mouse, "Have you read *Waverley*, Lady Selena?''

She appeared flattered at this slim attention. "I have been meaning to,'' she answered, and smiled. Mr. Beecham had lovely eyes, all soft and glowing. They didn't pierce right through like Harrup's, nor look so closely at your bosom, either. For his part, Ronald had the strangest sensation of hearing celestial music when he beheld the vision.

Her answer was sufficient encouragement for him to burst forth into raptures over Walter Scott. Diana poked Harrup's shoulder and when she had his attention told him her suspicions about Mrs. Whitby. He appeared interested. "I'll drop around tomorrow and see if she's there. Best say no more at this time,'' he cautioned, glancing to his fiancée.

Lady Selena was engrossed in Ronald's story of Edward Waverley and Rose Bradwardine. The complications of Hanoverians and Jacobites sounded confusing, but she listened to the soft-spoken young gentleman with the shy smile and was emboldened to tell him it sounded very exciting.

"You must read it," Ronald told her. "I'll lend my copy to you as soon as I've finished. Not later than tomorrow."

Lady Selena found no folly in this suggested time. "Will you finish it in one day?" she asked, batting her eyes in admiration.

"It's too good to put down. I didn't want to come here tonight. But I'm glad I did," he admitted. "The best of men cannot suspend their fate," he added with a curious smile.

Lady Selena blushed and glanced fearfully at Harrup, who displayed no evidence of jealousy. The curtain was rising. He turned aside and said "Hush" as though she were an infant. Selena obediently fell silent and turned her head to the stage.

When the audience roared with laughter, Selena smiled in confusion and thought this was rather a warm play for Harrup to have taken her to. When the first intermission came, Harrup offered to take the ladies out for wine. "Or you and Ronald can stay here, Di, and I'll have it brought in," he offered.

She was happy to sit and watch the audience move about. Ronald wasn't much company, but the wine was excellent, and the break passed quickly. She noticed Harrup had taken Lady Selena to visit another box. The gentlemen were ogling Selena, and Harrup stood like a proud father, preening himself at his conquest. They certainly made a handsome couple, she had to acknowledge that much.

They returned when the bell rang and took up their same seats as before during the second act. At the next intermission, Harrup turned to Diana and said, "Would you like to stretch your legs?"

"You've already shown your fiancée off. I guess your reputation can bear being seen with me."

"I was hoping to have some private conversation with you. I've discovered something of interest that I don't wish Lady Selena to hear.

"Excuse us. Miss Beecham wants to get some exercise," Harrup said to his fiancée before leaving.

Lady Selena breathed a sigh of relief and smiled at Ronald as the others left.

"She's here," Harrup said, as soon as they were out of the box.

"Who is? Mrs. Whitby?" Diana asked. Her eyes sparkled with interest.

"Yes, I spotted her at intermission. She's not with Markwell, but he's here, too. I expect they'll meet now. I'm sure she saw me—she knows where my box is—but she didn't once glance in my direction."

"She's ashamed to," Diana told him.

"I really begin to wonder if you're right about her. Now would be the perfect time to slip into her rooms and get the letters," he suggested.

"She wouldn't have left them there after what happened to Markwell's," Diana said. "Some people learn by experience."

"Thank you for that barb, but I never had the experience of being blackmailed before."

They ordered the wine and strolled through the throng, looking for their quarry. Both Mrs. Whitby and Markwell were spotted, but not together. Harrup knew it was ineligible to accost a lightskirt when he was accompanied by a young lady, but he tried to catch Mrs. Whitby's eye. After five minutes, he knew she was purposely avoiding him and assumed a guilty conscience was the reason.

"We might as well go back to our box," he suggested. "I shouldn't abandon Selena for too long."

"She's very beautiful," Diana said.

"Every head in the place turned when we were on the stroll. She's a little shy with strangers, of course. That's why she hasn't said much."

"Strangers! Surely you are not a stranger to her."

"I am, practically. I've never been alone with her except when I popped the question."

"Then you don't actually—I mean—it wasn't a question of being violently in love?" she asked hesitantly.

"Any man with an eye in his head would love her. Why, even Ronald was wagging his tail like a puppy. You must warn him not to cut me out." He laughed, and they returned to the box. Ronald had taken the seat beside Lady Selena, but he jumped to his feet immediately and nearly capsized Diana.

Harrup smiled at the unexpected animation on his fiancée's lovely face. For the first time he heard her laugh. A beautiful, gentle, silver tinkle. "Discussing the play?" he asked. "Marvelous, is it not?"

"Mr. Beecham was telling me about a novel," Lady Selena said.

Ronald started guiltily and began bustling about to show Diana her seat. For the next act he didn't even look at Selena or think of anything else but her. Diana whispered that Mrs. Whitby was present and pointed her out to Ronald, but he was so shortsighted he could barely see the print on a page and had no notion what he was looking at. His mind was occupied with other things. Harrup was a pretty raffish person to be offering marriage to a sweet, innocent girl like Lady Selena. Already that shy bud had let slip that her papa had arranged the match—she was sure she would come to care for Harrup in time, she had said wistfully, but her eyes told another story. She had agreed with him that Horace knew what he wrote when he wrote the phrase,

85

"The half of my own soul." Their eyes had met and held when he quoted it. She had seen the hair lift on her arms.

Ronald felt he ought to rescue her and appreciated the irony of his position. He was dependent on the good offices of the man who was going to marry the woman he loved. There was no doubt in his mind that what he felt for Selena was true love. He felt weak, his head floating high above his body. He knew instinctively, too, that Lady Selena didn't love Harrup. When she looked at Harrup, her eyes were like the eyes of a doe with the muzzle trained on her. It was a situation worthy of Mr. Scott.

He felt vaguely that some action was called for on his part to rescue Lady Selena and knew in his bones that he would do nothing. Virgil knew something about human nature, too. "We are not all capable of everything," he wrote. "Deep in her breast lies the silent wound" was another insight. But it was in his breast the wound would cut deepest when he stood outside St. George's on Hanover Square in a few months and watched with tears in his heart while his beloved married Lord Harrup.

Then he glanced at his sister. His papa had remarked more than once that Di should have been his son, for she was the real man of the family. She was very good at practical problems. As ignorant as a swan about anything that really mattered, of course—unlike Selena, who showed a real appreciation for the classics. Still, Di had rescued Harrup's letters. Now she must help him rescue Lady Selena.

Before Ronald was dropped off that night, he had arranged with the ladies that he and Diana would call on Lady Selena the next day to deliver *Waverley*. Harrup, the scoundrel, hadn't a word to say against it. In his colossal arrogance he didn't recognize the threat of a boy in love.

Chapter Six

Ronald labored long with his cravat and not at all with his conscience as he prepared for the visit to Lady Selena the next day. At Belgrave Square, Diana pondered how she would tell him she still hadn't broached the matter of his position to Harrup. She had suggested a glass of wine to Harrup after their arrival home the evening before, hoping to find an opportunity to do it. Harrup, however, had not been in a good mood. He would speak of nothing but Laura Whitby's snubbing him at the play and what that augured.

"The appointment is to be made any day now," he worried. "If she's come to London to make mischief for me, why the deuce doesn't she make her demands and have done with it?"

"Perhaps you were right all along," Diana said, "and she has no notion of bothering you. You'll have to call on her. It is the only way to set your mind at rest."

"I'll do it tomorrow," he decided.

Still trying to nudge her host into a good mood, Diana tried another tack. "Lady Selena is extremely beautiful. Your boasting didn't do her justice."

His manner relaxed visibly. "A truly charming girl—quiet and well behaved, too."

"I noticed heads turning at the theater," Diana said.

"On this occasion, I believe the cats were staring at you,

87

wondering who you might be. A new lady in town always generates a certain interest.''

"Especially when she appears under the auspices of Lord Harrup, I daresay. They probably took me for Lady Selena's doyenne.''

Harrup studied her, smiling, and said, ''And Ronald for your father. The boy was quite bowled over with Selena, was he not? She seems well disposed toward him as well. I never saw her so animated before. I would be grateful if you and Ronald would entertain her a little while you're in town. I ought to do my own courting, but till the appointment is made, I mean to show Eldon *et al* my nose is glued to the grindstone. One thing this Whitby affair has shown me is the value of having a young, innocent bride. I would never have to fear Selena is cutting up any rigs behind my back.''

"I shall undertake to keep a tight rein on Ronald," Diana offered.

Was this the moment to ask her favor? She was on the point of doing it when a much better idea occurred to her. Would Lady Selena not make an unexceptionable seconder in this affair? She seemed genuinely fond of Ronald. After a few days to further the acquaintance, Diana would mention Ronald was on the lookout for work, and Harrup would have two ladies pestering him. He'd give in to gain peace.

Once she had decided to delay her request, there was no further reason to remain downstairs, and she set her empty glass aside. "It was a lovely evening, Harrup. Thank you so much for taking Ronald and me to the play.''

"You're not leaving already?" he asked, surprised. "We've hardly seen each other today.''

"We had breakfast and dinner together. We were together at the play all evening. Short of gluing my nose to the grindstone beside yours, we could hardly have been more together if we were chained.''

"I mean alone together," he said unthinkingly. "It's

nice to have a mature lady to talk to about things. In London the mature ladies are either gossipy cats or hoping to make you their new cicisebeo. And with the young ladies, of course, a gentleman has to walk on eggs. A man couldn't have a rational conversation with any of them.''

"By which you mean an improper one, I suppose?" she quizzed.

"I mean both, or either. I *do* have a mind you know, as well as—"

"Yes, I know," she said quickly, with a frightened look at him.

"As well as *emotions*, Miss Beecham. I am not quite so farouche as to call a spade a spade—even to a country girl who knows a thing or two about spades."

"I am happy to hear you *do* observe some of the proprieties."

Eager to keep him in tune, Diana accepted another glass of wine. They talked of London and the country, of Mrs. Whitby and Lady Selena and Peabody, and of human nature in general, like old friends, laughing much and complaining not a little of petty annoyances. After half an hour Diana was tired and said so bluntly.

"I've prosed your ear off, and here you've been wanting all the time to get your beauty rest. You should have told me so, Di."

"Not at all. I'm not so obliging as you, Harrup. You are held up as a pattern card of obligingness at the Willows, you must know. Especially after you've just given Peabody one of those nice fat envelopes. Take one when you visit Mrs. Whitby and you'll turn her up sweet. I expect she has drawers full of diamond bracelets. Cash will save her a trip to the pawn shop."

"Me, too," he answered, and laughed.

"Surely your pockets aren't to let? You wouldn't have to lay your watch on the shelf, would you?"

89

"No, no. When a lady is out of favor, secondhand jewelry is good enough for her."

"That's how you treat your erstwhile friends, is it?"

"Only when they've mistreated me first."

Diana rose and Harrup got up to accompany her to the staircase. "It's you I should have thought of marrying," he said facetiously. "You would be a comfortable wife. You wouldn't cut up stiff at a husband's extramarital flirtations."

She gave him a sapient stare. "How little you know me! I would disembowel any husband of mine who dared to look at another lady. Why do you think I'm still single? I could have had a marriage of convenience. Like all ninnyhammers, I am holding out for a grand passion. I don't want to miss the anxiety of waiting home alone, the loving clatter of crockery over my husband's head, the pangs of jealousy, the agony of heartbreak."

"A grand passion?" he asked mockingly. "I have no personal experience in that area. I believe that, like happiness, you will find it illusory. You should stifle your romantic notions and settle for a good, comfortable marriage of convenience."

She shook her head. "Poor Harrup. And poor Lady Selena." She went slowly upstairs, sad for her friend. Harrup may be beyond romance, but Lady Selena—would she settle for a marriage of convenience?

Harrup returned to the saloon for another glass of wine. As he sat on alone, he considered her words. They were the naive notions of maidenhood, he thought. A city gentleman who had seen innumerable friends marry for love, only to endure the concomitant jealousies and agonies Di had mentioned, knew the wiser course. It did seem wrong that a fiancé felt no thrilling surge when he was alone with his beautiful bride-to-be, though. Selena was more enjoyable in company. He almost dreaded those looming periods when he must be alone with her, dragging a few words from her like a tooth drawer pulling recalcitrant teeth. No doubt she'd overcome her shyness in time.

Diana slept in the next morning after her late night and missed Harrup at breakfast. Some uneasiness hung about her as she ate alone. She worried about Mrs. Whitby and the letters; she was sad to consider Harrup's approaching marriage of convenience; she pondered Ronald's position, and spared not a single worry that her brother was planning to steal Lady Selena away. Ronald's passionate outburst when he arrived came as a complete shock to her.

He looked unlike himself, his eyes burning with intensity. "Di, what are we going to do about Lady Selena?" he demanded.

"Harrup suggested we entertain her a little while he is busy at work," she replied. "We might take her to Richmond Hill or for drives, shopping—that is the sort of thing to amuse her, I think."

"I don't mean that!" Ronald scoffed, eyes blazing in wrath. "How can we rescue her from Harrup?"

Diana stared, speechless for a moment. "What on earth are you talking about?" she demanded.

"She doesn't love him! She told me so—oh, not in words exactly, but the way she looks at him. Didn't you see the fear and revulsion in her eyes?"

"No, nor did I hear it in her voice. Of course, she hadn't two words to say for herself."

"Her father arranged the match. She hardly knows Harrup."

"Then I think she will be pleasantly surprised when she comes to know him. He will be a considerate, undemanding husband."

"The man's a libertine," Ronald asserted forcefully. "Only look what he has put us through in the few days you've been here. Sent you calling on a lightskirt."

91

"He didn't send me! He suggested Peabody send a footman. We went of our own accord."

"Writing that woman love letters! Getting me arrested."

"And bailing you out! I hope you haven't discussed any of this with Lady Selena?" she asked sharply.

"Of course not. I couldn't sully her ears with tales of such debauchery. She is such a sweet innocent. Do you know what she loves more than anything in the world, Di?"

Diana considered it a moment and said "Bonbons?" in a quelling way.

In the throes of passion, Ronald was immune to irony. "Kittens," he announced. "Selena has four kittens. Her favorite is a poor tabby who had his tail chewed off by a dog."

"That's very touching, Ronald, but you must not go imagining yourself in love with Lady Selena. She is engaged to Harrup. Think what it would do to your chances of an appointment if you put a spoke in his wheel."

Ronald groaned in disbelief. "Ladies have no conception of what is important in life. Do you think I'd let my career stand in the way of rescuing Lady Selena? I would carry her off to Gretna Green today if she'd have me, and damn the consequences."

"That would be most unwise."

When on unsure ground, Ronald usually resorted to quotations, as he did now. " 'The gods could hardly love and be wise.' "

"You are no god, or even a gentleman of independent means. I trust Lady Selena shows more sense. We are going to pay a very short visit to her, Ronald. You will give her those volumes you're clutching to your bosom. We shall have a glass of wine or a cup of tea, and we shall leave."

All Ronald heard was that they were going to pay the visit. He jumped to his feet, scattering volumes to left and right, but still got to the door before Diana had her bonnet and pelisse on. His sister inveighed all the way to Grosvenor Square against rescuing Lady Selena. She soon realized that threats of misery heaped on Ronald's head in the execution of his scheme were not only disregarded but actually welcomed, and changed her tactics to make Selena the victim.

"If you really care for the girl, you'll think of her welfare," she said severely. "Her reputation would be ruined if she jilted Harrup. All polite doors would be slammed in her face. Her own family would disown her. You would do her a great disservice if you put any ideas of elopement in her head, Ronald. Don't be so selfish. She'd hate you in the end."

Ronald looked chastened. "Each of us must live in his own hell," he said bleakly.

A shyly smiling Lady Selena sat awaiting them in her mama's gold saloon. Lady Groden took one look at her callers and decided Miss Beecham could play propriety, which left her free to call in the modiste. The only good thing that happened during the visit was that Ronald fell nearly as mute as Lady Selena once he was actually in her presence. Or perhaps it was the third party that accounted for the pall of silence. He tendered the novel. Lady Selena accepted it and thanked him.

"I finished it last night," Ronald said.

Diana decided she must put the visit on a respectable footing and said, "Harrup is sorry he cannot be here himself, Lady Selena. He is so very busy just now, making a good impression on Lord Eldon, you know."

Instead of answering, Lady Selena cast an imploring eye in Ronald's direction. "Are you seeing him this evening?" Diana asked.

"Oh, I hope n—I don't believe so," Lady Selena said, blushing at what had slipped out.

"It will be quite a feather in his cap, being named attorney general," Diana plodded on. Her aim was to paint the groom in glowing colors. Lady Selena listened sullenly to this conversation, which was very similar to her papa's persuasions.

"Ronald is trying to find some sort of position," Di said next, to highlight the difference in circumstances between the suitors. This generated a spark of interest from the reluctant bride. "He cannot go on living on nothing a year," she added. This was, of course, an exaggeration, but allowable in the circumstances.

"I have a dowry of twenty thousand," Lady Selena mentioned. She didn't look at Ronald, but there was that in her gentle voice that hinted it was entirely at his disposal.

"I can always go home to the Willows if I don't find a job," Ronald said, ostensibly to his sister, but he peeped from his pale eyes to see if Lady Selena was listening, as indeed she was.

He read encouragement of this subject and went on to describe the future nest, in classical allusions first, but soon switching to plain English for Selena's edification. "A lovely place. A whole row of willow trees droop over the stream behind the house. I often used to catch fish there— in the stream, I mean. There are six cats in the barn," he added. The would-be lovers exchanged a meaningful smile.

Wine and glasses had been placed on the sofa table right under the hostess's nose, but she seemed unaware of them. To divert the subject, Diana asked if she might have a glass of wine. Lady Selena poured and passed the glasses. The visit had lasted fifteen minutes but seemed much longer. Diana was just wondering if she might politely leave when some other visitors arrived. Lady Groden was called down, and Diana found herself drawn into the adult circle. She spared a glance to her brother and Lady Selena when the talk permitted and saw they got on much better without her. Lady Selena became quite lively as they pored together over the copy of *Waverley*.

The new callers made only a short visit, and when they

rose to leave, Diana rose, too. Lady Groden proved a more gracious hostess than her daughter. "I am so happy you called, Miss Beecham," she said, pressing Diana's fingers. "It is reassuring to know Selena will have a few friends when Harrup carries her off to the country."

"I cannot think you have any fears on that score, Lady Groden," Diana objected. "Harrup spends most of the year in London. He makes only fleeting visits home."

The mother looked at her daughter, a shadow of concern in her eyes. "I expect Selena will spend more time in the country," she said. "Once they begin to fill the nursery, I mean. Selena does not take well to city life, and Harrup will be so busy, he shan't have much time for her. I hope you and she will be good friends. Keep an eye on her for me." She smiled.

Diana felt a nearly overpowering urge to demand why Lady Selena was being made to marry Harrup. It was only civility that forbade it, but no such civility need hamper her from asking Harrup later. The Beechams left, and the carriage went first to take Ronald home.

Ronald turned a stiff face to his sister. "Well, I did what you said," he told her. "I kept my tongue between my teeth and didn't say a word against Harrup. I even said she must marry him. I felt like a murderer, Di. Selena didn't cry, but her eyes were glazed. I know she should be mine, but the gods think otherwise."

"I cannot imagine why her parents are pushing this match forward," she admitted.

"Because Harrup is Harrup, and for no other reason. What *I* cannot understand is why he insists on having her. Why must the wretched libertines always marry the sweet, innocent girls? It tickles their perverted fancy, like a cat playing with a mouse."

Diana said nothing. She would not encourage Ronald, but she felt morally bound to discuss the matter with Harrup. He could not be aware that Lady Selena disliked him.

How could he? She never said anything. It happened that Harrup was dining out that evening, so she waited up for him. It was ten o'clock when he came in, whistling. His carefree mood annoyed Diana, who had been pacing his study, racked with worry.

Harrup stuck his head in at the door, beaming a smile. "Oh, good, you waited up for me. You may congratulate me, Di!" he said, and came in.

"Harrup, you have been made attorney general!" she exclaimed, smiling. His announcement put everything else out of her mind.

"No, not yet, but I have seen Laura. I can stop worrying about the letters. She doesn't have them. She returned all of them she had kept."

"It's odd she didn't keep the two warmest ones, when she kept the others," she pointed out, unconvinced.

Harrup, smiling fondly, sat down and poured two glasses of wine. "She wanted to keep them, but when she was preparing to leave Hitchin, she decided the wiser course was to burn them, in case they went astray. Very considerate of her."

"Yes, very considerate," Di said, "incredibly considerate, and I mean that literally. You actually believe her?"

"You don't know Laura as I do," he said, looking into the distance. "She is the best—the most—a *civilized* woman is what I mean. Not the petty sort a man too often ends up with."

Diana narrowed her eyes at this unlikely story. "How much did you give her?"

"Five hundred," he admitted unblushingly.

"What had she to say about Markwell?"

"She was furious with him. He was with her when you called—she admitted it. She told him you were bringing the letters to me, and he left very shortly after. She had no idea he meant to steal them. She didn't know he *had* stolen them. He was her lover till today. That is why she is breaking with him. In fact, Laura and I may—oh, after the treacle moon is history, I mean," he added hastily, when he saw the wrath gathering on Diana's brow.

"You are despicable!" Diana hissed. "Ronald is right. Lady Selena, despite her muteness, is too good for you. Will you please tell me, Harrup, why you insist on marrying an innocent young girl who hates you?"

Harrup's merry mood evaporated. "What are you talking about?" he demanded angrily.

"You know perfectly well what I am talking about. Lady Selena doesn't love you, and you don't love her."

"The word you used was *hate*!"

"It comes to the same thing in the end. She's being forced into this marriage by her parents—her father, I suspect, since her mother is considerably worried."

"She is not being forced! I asked her to marry me—she said yes, without blinking. Her mother was grinning from ear to ear when we told her the news."

"Well, she's not grinning now. She asked me to look after Selena when you have abandoned her in the country. The fact of the matter is, you have decided your position requires the respectability of marriage and are willing to sacrifice that poor child—chosen because other men stare at her beauty. What kind of a creature are you?"

Harrup's face was white, his nostrils quivering indignantly. "Arranged marriages are nothing new under the sun. Now that you've given vent to your ill-bred piece of impertinence, Miss Beecham, perhaps you would deign to tell me what in my behavior has earned the word *despicable*?"

"I am talking about your bare-faced gall in standing there, telling me you plan to return to Mrs. Whitby after the honeymoon with Selena. I am perfectly well aware such things happen, but to plan them in advance of the wedding must surely be a new low in behavior, even for the likes of you."

"It was just a fleeting thought! I didn't say anything to Laura."

"You didn't give her five hundred pounds as an option on her future services, either, I suppose? Or continuing services," she added. "The wedding isn't for two months. A man of your kidney would hardly deprive himself of his lightskirt for so long!"

Harrup summoned all his dignity. "You take an overweening interest in my affairs!" he said coolly.

"No, I take no further interest whatsoever in your affairs. My only interest was to ingratiate you so you'd give Ronald a position. But it's not worth it. Ronald said so himself, and for once he's right. I shall be leaving in the morning. Common decency compels me to warn you Ronald is in love with Selena, and I believe the feeling is mutual. I sincerely hope she turns you off."

His dark eyes glowed dangerously. "Have you been running to her with tales of my doings? You have the audacity to accept my hospitality and repay it in this manner? Do you think Groden is unaware of my character? Do you *really* believe any gentleman in my position is much different? Groden approached me with the idea. I didn't go after his daughter. He knew I wanted a wife; he wanted a match for her. It's a business agreement that I have every intention of fulfilling. Selena wouldn't give a tinker's curse if I had a dozen mistresses. I daresay she'd welcome them."

"No doubt that would be preferable to your lovemaking, but why should she have to settle for the lesser of two evils? She hasn't done anything to deserve this. A young and trusting daughter is not a piece of merchandise to barter with. She may have lacked the gumption to object before she came to know you. I think you'll find the girl has changed, now that she's been exposed to a few hours of your attentions. You were wise to try to shimmy out of even that token show of respect to your future wife, Har-

98

rup. You chose the wrong substitute in Ronald, however. He loves Selena, you see. It's a condition that occasionally afflicts real people. I don't believe it's contagious, so you need not fear contamination.''

Diana rose and strode angrily toward the door. ''And I didn't let Ronald say a word against you, either,'' she said over her shoulder, just before slamming the door.

She knew sleep was impossible and didn't even bother undressing when she had closed her bedroom door behind her. She paced to and fro, thinking of a dozen other things she should have said, yet half regretting she had said so much. But really it was unconscionable for Harrup to marry Selena. Not that Groden would let her cry off, and certainly not for a mere squire's son like Ronald. It was a hopeless situation. She wished she could pack up her bag and leave that very night. At least she could warn Peabody they'd be leaving early in the morning.

She went to the adjoining door and tapped lightly. A muffled voice told her to come in. A small lamp burned beside Peabody's bed. On the pillow Peabody's cap moved restlessly.

''I hope I didn't awaken you?'' Diana said.

''I'm not sleeping, Di. I have got one of my earaches. I was out in the garden with Mrs. Dunaway this afternoon looking for a corner where she could plant some herbs, and the wind got at me.''

''Oh, dear! I hope it isn't very bad.''

''I think if I take some laudanum I might find a few minutes' sleep.''

''I'll ask Mrs. Dunaway if she has some.''

Diana went in search of the housekeeper and found her in her parlor. ''Here you go, dear. Be sure you bring back the bottle. I may need a drop myself. The wind didn't bother my ears, but my knees are aching like a bad tooth. It's the rheumatism.'' She sighed.

After Peabody was settled in, Diana said, ''Do you think

you'll be fit to travel tomorrow, Peabody? I hoped to get an early start.''

"Tomorrow? You forget Harrup has asked us to stay a week. I thought you were looking forward to it.''

"I've quarreled with him. I'd really like to leave.''

"Can you never behave properly? What happened?'' Peabody demanded.

"It's his marrying Selena. I cannot like it. He shouldn't marry her.''

"It's a match made in heaven,'' Peabody replied.

"No, made in the House of Lords. I'm afraid I've put Harrup in a pelter.''

"Pshaw. It will have blown over by the morning.''

Diana didn't think the quarrel would dissipate so quickly, but she hoped the earache would. She went back downstairs with Mrs. Dunaway's laudanum, and as she approached the stairs to return to her room, Harrup came into the hall.

"I'd like to speak to you for a moment, Diana,'' he said.

His mood was milder now. Not only had the anger vanished, but a shadow of apology colored his voice. "What is it?'' she asked curtly.

He showed her into his office, and they both sat down. "I have behaved poorly to a guest and dear friend. I want to apologize, and urge you not to go darting off before your visit is completed.''

Diana compared the conciliating words with the stiff face that was speaking them and chose a moderate course. "I may have to remain another day. Peabody has one of her earaches. I was just returning Mrs. Dunaway's laudanum.''

He gave a rueful smile. "Here I thought you were making an excuse to come downstairs to patch up our quarrel.''

"No, but I daresay I said more than I ought, and I am sorry I said it. Which doesn't mean I take it back.''

"If that is an apology,'' he said doubtfully, "you are

forgiven. I'm not such an ogre as you think, you know. I had no idea Selena actively disliked me. 'Hate' is a strong word. I must know if it came from Selena herself.''

"It's Ronald's word, actually. 'Fear' and 'revulsion' were a couple of others. I *do* think the girl is afraid of you.''

He shrugged. "There's no reason for her to be. I've never said a cross word to her in my life.''

"Have you taken the time and trouble to say any *kind* ones?'' she asked gently. "She's young, Harrup. Naturally she's frightened to be pitched into marriage with an older gentleman she scarcely knows from Adam.''

"If she doesn't marry me, she'll marry someone like me. I know she has always feared her father, and perhaps I've fallen under his shadow. Groden would never permit Selena to marry Ronald. He's ambitious. He married all his daughters off to noblemen. He won't permit her to jilt me at all, and a gentleman can hardly call off the match. I want you to know I intend to allay Selena's fear, hatred, and revulsion before the wedding. I shall make a marked effort in that direction. You'll see.'' He smiled. "I'll bring her round my thumb. It's not only lightskirts I can charm. A woman is a woman.''

"Then I'm happy I spoke to you. It was worth it if it makes Selena's future life a little easier. Her mama would be happy with me. Already I'm looking out for her daughter. I find satisfaction in it, too,'' she mused.

"Take care, or you'll end up a maiden aunt, Di, mothering everyone else's children. What you ought to do is get busy and have some of your own.''

"What I ought to do is go to bed,'' she said wearily.

A satirical gleam shone in Harrup's eyes and he replied, "That is the first step, certainly.''

Diana shook her head. "You're incorrigible, Harrup.''

"I'm not, you know. I just never found a stern lady to

correct my evil ways. No one ever ripped up at me so violently before.''

An image of Selena's mild face flashed into Diana's mind. "And never will again," she said.

"What, have you given up on me? I think I might be tamed with a little persistence.''

She remembered Selena and her kittens. "You're not my tiger, thank goodness.''

When Diana glanced up, Harrup was gazing at her steadily. There was a peculiar, concentrated look in his eyes. An air of surprise, somehow. Her glass was empty, and she refilled it, still with his dark eyes following her, making her self-conscious. She swished the wine around in the glass, watching the reflected light swirl. "Selena likes kittens, Harrup. Did you know that? She has no use for tigers. Why don't you give her a kitten? She'd love it.''

He hesitated a moment before speaking, and when he spoke, his voice was low. "A leopard can't change his spots, and I expect a tiger doesn't lose his stripes without a good deal of effort, but I shall try. I'll buy Selena a kitten. What color would she like?''

"Need you ask? White, of course.''

"Of course.''

"If it has lost an ear or eye, so much the better.''

"A collector of strays, is she? No wonder Ronald appeals to her. Speaking of Ronald, what position is it he wants?''

Ronald's working for Harrup no longer appeared feasible, given the circumstances of Selena's being forever between them. "Something that will keep his nose in a book. He's intelligent, Harrup. He would make an abominable M.P. or anything that requires public appearances, but as a speech writer or research man for policy decisions, he would be ideal.''

"I thought he would take over the Willows.''

"Papa's only fifty,'' she pointed out. "After the expense

102

of a university education, Ronald is expected to add a few baubles to the family tree. Anything you could do would be appreciated.''

He looked at her askance. ''For that you had to ingratiate me? That's not an extraordinary request from a neighbor.''

''Well, to tell the truth, it was your special assistant we had in our eye, but now that he's decided he loves Selena, it's not a good idea for him to be too much in your pocket.''

Harrup rubbed his chin thoughtfully. ''Very true. That would provide a dangerous proximity to my fiancée. Lady Groden is not entirely pleased with the match, I think you intimated?''

''She seemed worried. You will be kind to Selena, won't you, Harrup? I think if Selena is happy, Ronald won't do anything foolish. He mentioned Gretna Green, but really he is much too passive to try anything of the sort. He'd end up asking me to hire the carriage and come along to chaperon them.''

Diana finished her wine and left, happy to have made it up with Harrup and relieved that he wasn't really so bad. Harrup sat drumming his fingers on his desk, wearing a pensive expression. What had gotten into him to tell Di his vagrant thoughts about returning to Laura? It was no more than that, a passing thought. He was treating Di as if she were one of his cronies—he must remember she was a young lady, and one with a temper that didn't balk at tackling a tiger.

Chapter Seven

Diana did not awaken early in the morning. It wanted only ten minutes of eight when she opened her eyes. It immediately darted into her head that if she hurried, she might catch Harrup before he left for the office. She bounded from bed and scrambled into her gown. It was while she sat in front of the mirror brushing her hair that she asked herself why she was in such a panic to see him before he left. She had nothing in particular to say to him. They had had a long cose the night before. All the little wrinkles between them were once more ironed out to their mutual satisfaction, yet something in her was eager to run downstairs with her hair still in tangles and see him.

She could find no cause for her eagerness. It was just a vague feeling that she wanted to see him again before— what? She would see him at dinner. Her hasty departure was no longer spoken of. But at dinner they would not be alone—possibly they would not even be together. Harrup might dine out with Lady Selena and the Grodens. She hastened to the head of the stairs and was about to set her foot on the first step when she heard Harrup taking his leave of the butler.

"I'm off, Stoker. Say good morning to Miss Beecham for me. Tell her—oh, never mind. I'm not sure I'll be able to return for luncheon. Make sure that she and Miss Peabody are comfortable and have whatever they desire.''

Stoker mumbled a reply, and Harrup left. Diana returned to her room feeling cheated. She had missed him—he would probably not be home for luncheon. She wouldn't see him till evening. A whole long day to be got in, somehow. At least, Harrup had left a secondhand "good morning" for her. He had been thinking of her. Diana was reluctant to look into her reasons for the feeling of emptiness that was within her.

She went to see how Peabody's earache was progressing, only to learn her chaperon was still afflicted with some pain.

"I shan't stay in bed all day, Diana," Peabody told her, "but pray do not expect me to go out of doors, with that hard London wind blowing. It is the nasty Thames that fills the air with moisture and does the mischief. I pray Ronald escapes it. You must send a note off and ask him to take you about the city."

Diana made sympathetic sounds, but she found no pleasure in a contemplation of seeing London with Ronald. Again she asked herself why. Her occasional trips to London were the highlights of a dull life. This one was proving more interesting than usual. Life was sumptuous under Harrup's roof, despite their quarrels. A quarrel was not something Diana ever dreaded. And still she hesitated to look into the cause for her gloom.

Her mind skated around the issue while she took breakfast alone. Unhappiness with Harrup's coming marriage to Lady Selena certainly accounted for a part of her mood. It was an ineligible match in all but rank and wealth. With the best of intentions and some effort on his part, it might be a decent marriage, but it would never be a good one. Two more unsuited persons would be difficult to find, and Ronald would suffer into the bargain. Had she become a philanthropist over night, permitting the potential grief of others to cast her into the dismals? She was too honest to accept such an edifying picture of herself. She was just jealous of Lady Selena. She wanted to be Harrup's bride herself, to stand beside the attorney general and share in some small degree his honors, his work.

This interpretation didn't sit easily, either. If she were prey to a hankering for rank and riches, she would have been aware of it before her twenty-fifth year. No, the dreadful truth was that she was jealous of Laura Whitby. It wasn't Harrup's title and money she wanted; it was his admiration, his company when he was at leisure, his love. She had enjoyed their private meetings, their arguments, had felt the sting of jealousy before this moment. It wasn't for Lady Selena that she had taken him to task about his postmarital plans for Mrs. Whitby. Last night she had been angry for herself—that was why she'd attacked so violently. He must think she was an interfering shrew.

When had it happened? When had she been fool enough to fall in love with a man who was in love with a lightskirt, and engaged to another lady besides? Either circumstance should have been enough to open her eyes. It had sneaked up and caught her unawares. It was the fact of Harrup's being already attached that had brought down their defenses. Neither had bothered to put on the polite face of courting, and in the ensuing free-for-all, she had come to love a man with all his human weaknesses laid bare.

Harrup was no hero. He was arrogant, ambitious, addicted to the fair sex. Lady Selena would not have an easy life with him—but she would have an interesting life. Except that the silly chit wouldn't know enough to realize it was interesting. She wouldn't know how to control Harrup's vices, or even want to try. And they could be controlled if his wife wielded a firm hand. Harrup wasn't completely incorrigible; he just needed someone to nag him into rectitude.

While these thoughts filled Diana's head, the door knocker sounded and Ronald was shown in.

"I don't suppose you spoke to Harrup about a position for me?" he asked.

"The subject arose, but nothing definite has been settled. He'll certainly find something for you, Ronald. I did take him to task about Lady Selena, however. He has agreed to show her every kindness in the future. I'm sure he can conciliate her if he puts his mind to it."

This speech didn't have the expected result. Rather than thanking her, Ronald looked displeased at her interference. "She will never be happy married to that old man," he said firmly. "They haven't a single thing in common. 'To like and dislike the same things, that is indeed true friendship.' I would add 'and true love' to the quotation."

"But she *will be* married to him, Ronald, and at least she will not be made unhappy."

Ronald accepted a cup of coffee, and while he was nursing it, Stoker appeared at the door.

"Lady Groden and Lady Selena are waiting in the saloon, Miss Beecham," he said.

Diana looked startled. "Did you not tell them Lord Harrup is out?" she asked.

"They are calling on yourself, ma'am."

"Oh, dear!" she exclaimed, and looked to Ronald for assistance.

She didn't know whether the pink flush rising up from his collar denoted simple pleasure or a guilty foreknowledge of this visit. Had he arranged it the day before? How had he got Lady Groden to connive with him? Diana was in a quandary. She had warned Ronald, she had warned Harrup; must she now go so far as to warn Lady Selena's mama? While she silently debated this, Ronald rose and flew off to the saloon. When Diana arrived a few paces behind him, he had already detached Lady Selena and was leading her to a loveseat away from her mama.

Diana welcomed the callers, waiting expectantly to hear what had occasioned this unexpected visit. "You have heard the news?" Lady Groden asked. A broad smile sat on the dame's face.

For one absurd moment, Diana thought she was going to say Lady Selena had called off the wedding. She was trembling like a *blanc-manger* when she replied, "No, ma'am. I don't know what you are talking about."

"Harrup has received his appointment. Groden wrote me a note from Westminster this morning. It is being announced as soon as the House sits today."

Diana was happy for Harrup, but her overall reaction was one of disappointment. "I am so happy to hear it," she said. Her eyes turned to Lady Selena to see how that young lady was taking the news. Selena was gazing silently at Ronald. No conversation passed between them, but their eyes said much. *Now they will surely make me have him*, Diana interpreted from the strained face that stared imploringly at her brother.

"Harrup will doubtlessly be sending a note home as soon as he has a moment," Lady Groden continued. "I have several calls to make, and could not wait for you to hear from him. Groden desires me to have a celebration party this evening. Dinner is all I can arrange on such short notice. I hope you and your brother will join us."

"We would be very happy to accept," Diana said.

"Excellent. I shall be making my calls in person, as time is short. Will you come with me, Selena, or would you rather remain and visit with Miss Beecham?" the mother asked.

"Oh, I am sure Lady Selena will want to accompany you," Diana said swiftly.

Lady Selena cast an angry eye at her hostess. "I would rather remain for a visit, Mama. If Miss Beecham has no objection," she said.

Miss Beecham sought in vain for a valid objection. "My

108

chaperon is not feeling well today. I'm afraid I am confined to the house," she ventured.

Lady Groden laughed inanely. "Mr. Beecham is chaperon enough for you two ladies if you wish to go out," she said, as she rose and pulled on her gloves. "Remember, Selena, you have the coiffeur coming at two."

Diana glanced at the head-and-shoulders clock on the mantelpiece. It was only ten o'clock—an unusually early hour for a social call, and one that left her four hours to ride herd on Ronald and Selena. Her heart sank at the prospect of such a daunting chore. For the next four hours she did not leave their sides for a moment. She had Harrup's carriage called and took them to every park in the city and half the churches. She insisted on seeing St. Paul's and the Tower of London and the Elgin Marbles on display at Somerset House.

If she turned her back for a moment during any of these diversions to look at a gargoyle or turret, she found the two young lovers whispering when she turned back. By one-thirty her head ached and her feet were tired, but the unwanted guest still lingered. Shyness, she had learned, was not so great a part of Selena's makeup as she'd thought. The girl was forward enough when she was off the leash. It was her soft voice that led one astray.

Finally Diana said bluntly, "You had best go home now, Lady Selena. The coiffeur will be waiting for you."

"I'll see you tonight, Ronald," Lady Selena said softly, love gleaming in her eyes.

"Till this evening," Ronald answered.

"I'm taking you home now, Ronald," Diana said when they were alone. "And don't ever play such a wretched stunt on me again. Have you no scruples, to be making up to Harrup's fiancée behind his back, when he is arranging a position for you?"

Ronald drew a deep sigh. "We only have these few days together, Diana. You can count on my honor and my discretion. I would never do anything to discredit Selena, but

109

we must have these few hours to remember. It is not too much to ask of fate.''

''My God, you sound like Peabody.''

She left Ronald off at his flat and went directly home, planning to check up on Peabody. Stoker met her in the hallway. ''His lordship made a darting visit home to tell you of his appointment, Miss Beecham. He was very sorry to miss you.''

Diana's heart plunged deeper in her chest to hear she'd missed him. ''How thoughtful of him.'' She smiled wanly. ''Miss Peabody will be delighted with the news. I must tell her.''

''He left a note,'' Stoker added, and handed her a piece of folded paper.

Diana went to her room to read it.

Dear Heart: Have a very large bottle of champagne and two glasses prepared to celebrate the victory. There is only one shadow to this day.

Her heart thudded heavily, and she closed her eyes for a moment, fearful to read on. Was he going to say he regretted his betrothal? She opened her eyes and read.

Markwell looks like the cat that just swallowed the canary. Unsettling, *n'est-ce pas*? Perhaps we are not finished with Whitby and the billets-doux yet. Best stand prepared for another break-in. Your deliriously happy attorney general, Harrup.

There was much in the note to please her and much to cause concern. ''Dear Heart'' was an opening that allowed any amount of pleasant conjecture. The absence of Lady Selena's name told her nothing, but she worried about Markwell's gloating mood. Was it possible he and Mrs.

110

Whitby still held the other two letters, the most incriminating ones? Why would they wait so long to use them?

She went to tell Peabody the news. "Dear Chuggie! I knew he would succeed." Peabody smiled. "He is like a dog with a bone when he wants something. He allows nothing to stand in his way."

"I am very happy for him," Diana said, forcing her smile to match the dimensions of Peabody's.

"I believe I shall just nip down and speak to Mrs. Dunaway," Peabody decided. "The oil of cinnamon has done wonders for my ear. We must prepare a very special dinner for Harrup."

"The Grodens are having a dinner party, Peabody."

"Ah, then we shall miss it." She sighed.

"Lady Groden invited Ronald and myself."

"Did she, indeed?" Peabody asked, gratified at this attention to her two pets.

"Why don't you stay in bed and rest?" Diana suggested.

"I am feeling much better now. I'll stuff cotton wool in my ears and go downstairs. There is nothing so tedious as being forced into bed all day long, sipping pap like an invalid."

Peabody dressed and went to celebrate with Mrs. Dunaway. Diana had lunch alone and spent a fairly dull afternoon in Harrup's library, thinking and worrying. She deduced that Mrs. Whitby had purposely kept the two most incriminating letters till after Harrup's appointment so that he would pay more dearly for them. An attorney general would be more jealous for his reputation than a mere member of the Privy Council, and more easily bled. How could she help Harrup recover his letters?

This was the subject that creased her brow when she looked up and saw Harrup standing in the doorway, gazing at her from his dark eyes. He wasn't smiling, but there was a look of contentment in his expression.

111

"Harrup! When did you get home? I didn't hear you come in," she exclaimed.

"I just arrived. No champagne? I thought you might have begun the celebrations early."

"No, I was waiting for you." He entered and rang for the champagne.

"Congratulations," Diana said.

She felt suddenly shy of him. The old ease was gone, leaving her self-conscious and uncertain. Nor did Harrup help matters. He, too, seemed ill at ease, as though aware of her feelings. Perhaps he even shared them. His eyes would rest too long on her, then dart away suddenly. She sensed a wariness, an uncertainness of how he ought to behave. Diana decided it was ridiculous for two mature friends to be so gauche and forced herself to act normally when the champagne arrived.

"Did Markwell say anything?" she asked.

"No, but his gloating phiz has got my nerves on edge. I believe I've figured out why Whitby delayed dunning me."

"Yes, so have I. The attorney general will bleed more freely."

"Precisely. Part of the reason I left early was to follow Markwell when he left Westminster. He went to Hyde Park and met Mrs. Whitby. The two of them were laughing like hyenas."

"Oh, dear! That does look bad."

"When I realized Mrs. Whitby wasn't home, I dropped around to her flat, hoping to get in somehow. There was a servant there—I know her servants and tried my hand at bribing her dresser."

Diana looked interested. "Any luck?"

"The woman was amenable to bribery. She told me Mrs. Whitby has some papers she always keeps on her person. Two letters," he added, lifting a brow at this significant fact.

"On her person? Do you mean in her reticule?" Diana asked. Already she was figuring when and where would be the optimum moment to snatch the purse.

"No, secreted in her bosom."

"Oh. Then I can be no help. You'll have to try your luck again, Harrup," she added, a mischievous smile lighting her eyes.

"It's too late for that. The bosom, I fear, is closed to me forever."

"Do you think the dresser might . . ."

"Short of knocking Mrs. Whitby on the head and stealing them, I don't see how she could help. She's as venal as Whitby. I imagine her mistress knows of my visit by now."

Diana drew a deep sigh. "In that case, precautions will be taken while Mrs. Whitby sleeps, too. It looks hopeless."

"Yes, there's always a serpent in the garden. And I hear the Grodens have laid a party on for this evening as well."

"Lady Groden was here this morning—with Lady Selena," Diana told him. She watched him closely and saw no light of interest at hearing the lady's name.

"I forgot to inquire how you had spent your day," Harrup said, and settled back to hear her story.

"I hadn't meant to burden you with that. You have enough problems."

"What happened?" he asked with quickening interest.

"Nothing of any account. Lady Selena decided to remain here when her mama left. I toured London with her for four hours. Ronald was with me. I half suspect the two of them had prearranged the meeting, though I don't see how. I spoke to Ronald, and he assured me he has no ungentlemanly intentions of cutting you out. It is just that they want to store up a few romantic memories to brighten their dim future. You must be very nice to Lady Selena

113

this evening. I don't suppose your busy day left you time to find a kitten?''

Harrup shook his head. ''No. I was half afraid you might have done it for me. That is—I thought you might have done it, for a joke, you know.''

It was the word *afraid* that set him off on that awkward explanation. They both knew it, and the knowledge that Harrup didn't really want to conciliate his fiancée sat between them like a cocked pistol, making them nervous.

Diana blushed prettily and said, ''I let you down. Where would one procure a white kitten in London?''

''I'll be damned if I know.''

He poured another glass of champagne, and they sat on together, talking. ''I will be expected to have a party to celebrate my new honor,'' he mentioned.

''You'll wait till you hear from Mrs. Whitby?''

Harrup rubbed his chin distractedly. ''I don't know what to do. I'll look like a fool if those letters are printed. I believe I shall just go on as if there were nothing the matter, and when Whitby duns me, I'll pay up. It serves me right for being such an egregious ass.''

''You haven't done anything worse than plenty of other gentlemen.''

He shook his head ruefully. ''Oh, yes, I have. I was indiscreet enough to get caught. A man can get away with doing and saying things he should never put on paper. I'm a babe in the woods, and here you thought me an experi-. enced villain.''

''At least you were a bachelor, not even engaged when you wrote them,'' she pointed out.

''I'm engaged now. Groden is one of the few lords who takes high ground on moral matters, too—at least in public. His choosing me for a son-in-law indicates my character isn't completely blackened,'' he pointed out.

''Only a little tattered around the edges. Well, it seems there's nothing to be done, so I shall dress for dinner.''

"Let's finish the champagne," he suggested, but when he lifted the bottle, it was empty.

Diana laughed. "You didn't think I'd walk away if there were any left!" she teased. "It wasn't your scintillating conversation that held me. Papa never has champagne at home."

"My champagne thanks you for that compliment."

As Diana's striped lutestring was beyond repair, she was left with no choice but to wear her blue satin to the Grodens' party. An off-the-shoulder satin gown with silver ribbons beneath the bodice and a ruched skirt would have been considered too ornate for a simple dinner party in the country. She feared that with such a stickler as Lord Groden she might be considered overdressed, even in London. When she had arranged her hair and added her pearl-and-diamond earrings, she went below to ask Harrup's opinion.

He awaited her in the saloon, pacing and looking from staircase to clock. When he heard her tread, he went to the doorway. Diana stopped beneath the chandelier, a slender, graceful form. Her golden hair gleamed like a crown on her proud head. Prisms of painted rainbows reflected on her shoulders and gown from the overhead crystals. She looked at him uncertainly, wondering at his peculiar expression. He wasn't smiling, yet she read no condemnation in his eyes.

"Do I look hopelessly provincial, Harrup?" she asked bluntly. "I destroyed my lutestring and have nothing else to wear. When one is overdressed for the occasion, she looks so dreadfully underbred. What do you think?" she asked, and did a slow pirouette.

Harrup came forward and took her hand to lead her into the saloon. "Unexceptionable. You'll put them all in the shade."

"Lady Groden, perhaps. I'll hardly cast a shadow on Lady Selena's beauty."

"Some gentlemen prefer roses to buds," he said, running his eyes over her from head to toe in an assessing way.

She disliked such close scrutiny and snipped at him. "I only want an opinion on the suitability of the gown. Is it too décolleté?"

His dark eyes examined the area under consideration till she felt quite warm. "Certainly not for my taste," he assured her. "And the color suits you. I erred in calling Laura's eyes star sapphires. It is yours that resemble the jewel."

Such heavy-handed flattery as this could only be treated as a joke. "I don't suppose you'd care to put it in writing?" she quipped.

A spontaneous burst of laughter came from Harrup. It was a natural sound, unlike the sardonic mirth she was more accustomed to hearing from him. "I've gone beyond the acceptable limit of complimenting, have I?" he asked.

"When the eyes become jewels and the lips rosebuds, a lady knows she is dealing with a gazetted flirt—and a demmed unoriginal one to boot."

"The gazetted flirt I can forgive, but unoriginal? Cut to the quick, Miss Beecham."

Before more could be said, the door knocker sounded and Ronald was admitted. His arrival reminded Diana that her brother's job was still unsettled. She looked hopefully to Harrup, who was regarding Ronald closely.

Diana followed his gaze, trying to see Ronald as an outsider would. Beside Harrup, he looked extremely unprepossessing. Slight in stature, young, the jacket not of the first stare or even of the second, and one glove already dropped on the floor. Poor Ronald. He looked like an unlicked cub, and it struck her as unfair that he should make such a poor appearance when he was actually very intelligent. To add to the rest, Ronald wore a sulky expression, due to his rampant jealousy of Harrup.

"Congratulations, Harrup. I hear you got the position," Ronald said.

"Thank you. Later this evening we must decide what post best suits your abilities," Harrup replied.

This hopeful remark brought a smile to both the Beechams' faces. It was in this cheerful mood that the carriage embarked for Lord Groden's house.

Chapter Eight

The atmosphere at the Groden residence had changed noticeably from Diana's last visit, and she soon deduced that the cause of the change was Lord Groden. There was a formality, a stiffness bordering on hostility in his manner. Lord Groden was a fierce-looking old gentleman with snow-white hair and bushy gray eyebrows. He wore a habitual scowl and spoke gruffly. Though he was trying to smile on this occasion, it was such an unusual expression for him that he had only indifferent success.

As soon as the preliminaries had been accomplished—introductions and congratulations to the new attorney general—Groden turned a piercing gaze on the newcomers. Neighbors and friends of his future son-in-law were of some slight interest. To Groden, a lady was no more than an ornament and a potential bride for someone. He tacitly acknowledged that Miss Beecham fulfilled her ornamental function adequately, and as he had no unmarried sons, her dowry didn't interest him. It was Ronald Beecham whose bona fides must be established before he was made welcome under his roof.

"My gel tells me you are just down from Oxford and looking about for a position," he said accusingly to Ronald.

Ronald shifted uneasily in his chair. "Yes, sir," he murmured.

"Speak up, lad."

"Yes, sir," Ronald said, too loudly this time.

"What sort of work is it you have in mind?"

"All work is noble," Ronald answered simply.

Groden drew his monumental gray eyebrows together and stared. "Shoveling out a stable ain't noble, sir. Nor proper work for a university lad, either. You're a Tory at least, I take it?"

"The Beechams have always been Tories," Harrup informed the host.

The gray brows eased to mere hostility. "Are you interested in government at all?" he asked Ronald.

Ronald glanced at Selena, who nodded her encouragement. "Any man who isn't interested in the body that exercises control over his life is a fool. I hope I am not a fool, sir."

"Aye, there is something in that." Groden nodded, satisfied to hear his work described so properly. "The Tories have ruled for many a long year now, and mighty fine control they have exercised, too."

"As Aristotle says, they should rule who are able to rule best," Ronald announced, then added modestly, "I do not mean to say I see my role as a ruler, but as a handmaiden to rulers."

Harrup saw Groden furrowing his brow—it would be that "handmaiden" that did it—and spoke up to protect the hapless boy. "Something can be found for Mr. Beecham in my office."

"Do you know anything about the law?" Groden asked Ronald.

"Not much specific detail, but I know that law is order, and good law is good order. I would be happy to be a cog in the wheel of lawmaking. Again referring to Aristotle,

'For the things we have to learn before we can do them, we learn by doing them.' "

"You'll not find Parliament to be much like Aristotle's Utopia," Groden warned him.

"Actually Plato wrote the *Republic*, sir. I was quoting Aristotle's *Nicomachean Ethics* just now. The *Republic* is interesting, but too idealistic ever to work."

Ronald continued with various learned notions on the importance of politics and law. Groden was not a literary man himself, but he knew the value of a quotation and said to Harrup, "I daresay the lad could dress up a speech with all the trimmings. We could use a good speech writer. And the boy's politics are sound. 'Even when laws have been written down, they ought not always to remain unaltered.' There is a useful bit for changing our minds on the Corn Laws."

Lady Selena, resplendent in a pale blue gown with white underskirt, smiled softly at Ronald. Words of praise from her papa were rare. Before long, the small party had broken up into three discrete groups. Groden and Harrup sat talking in one corner, Ronald and Selena in another, and Diana and Lady Groden in a third. It was a fairly wretched party, both the conversation and food heavy. The best part of it was that it broke up early. Diana observed that Harrup and Selena didn't exchange a single private word, nor even those speaking, secret smiles that might be expected between a betrothed couple.

She took Harrup to task for it after they had delivered Ronald home. "You were supposed to conciliate your young bride this evening, sir," she reminded him. "I didn't see you put yourself out to do it."

"I'm only flesh and blood. Could *you* make love to anyone under the eye of that father?"

"Indeed I could not. I felt as though we had wandered into a spinster's wake. You might as well get used to it;

you will spend many such lively evenings after you're shackled.''

Harrup felt a shiver run down his spine, as though someone had just walked over his grave. What an appalling prospect! "And you haven't met the brothers and sisters yet," he said bleakly.

Diana laughed lightly. "I don't know how Ronald could remember quotations in such a setting. You must get Lady Selena away from them—take her out for some drives—and get to know her."

"Yes, I should, but first I must deal with Mrs. Whitby."

"Why don't we take a spin down Glasshouse Street and see if she's home?" Diana suggested.

"What's the point in that?" he asked, yet he felt strongly inclined to drive past her house himself.

"Merely to satisfy vulgar curiosity. I feel the need of some common vulgarity after our evening of overwhelming propriety. We could peek in Markwell's window—see if they're together."

Harrup pulled the check string and directed his driver to turn left into Glasshouse Street. He and Diana alighted and walked along arm in arm till they reached the house. Markwell's rooms were in darkness, but that was of no use to them. Overhead, lights gleamed in nearly every room of Mrs. Whitby's flat. Sounds of revelry—music and loud laughter—indicated that she was having a party.

"I wonder who's invited," Diana mused.

"Short of loitering in the shadows till two or three to watch them leave, I don't know how we can find out."

"I do!" Diana said, and laughed.

"We are not crashing that party," Harrup said very firmly.

"I am not that encroaching!" she defended. "What I had in mind was George Cuthbert. He has taken the flat next door. Let us see if he's home. We could peek out his door or just listen from his saloon. The voices can be heard from the street. You might recognize some accents from right next door."

"I'm not really that interested."

"Come on." She had already pulled him up the walk. "If men from your department are in league with Markwell, you must want to know," she pointed out.

They entered the hallway and started mounting the stairs. As they were halfway up, a door at the top opened, and two laughing voices were heard heading to the stairway. Harrup turned and fled down to hide himself behind the steps. The celerity of his departure left Diana stranded. She moved aside and smiled as two bucks a little the worse for drink came lumbering down. Hoping to recognize them from her visit to the House of Lords, she searched their faces closely. One was young and not unhandsome; the other an elderly gentlemen, stout, red-faced, nearly bald, but exceedingly elegant. Her perusal was all the encouragement they needed.

"I think we must return to Laura's rout if this little ladybird has come to entertain," the elderly gentleman suggested. His bold grin set her nerves on edge.

The younger man reached out an unsteady hand and pulled aside her cape to view her charms. Her eyes fiery, she snatched the cloak back and kicked his shin. "Get your hands off me, you fop!"

The elderly man reached for her arm, but before he could grasp it, she turned and pelted downstairs, just as Harrup's head appeared around the corner of the staircase. In the split second it took her to find shelter, she got a glimpse of Harrup's face, white with fury, eyes blazing like live coals. The two bucks were following closely at her heels.

She frisked to safety behind Harrup and missed the first blow, but she saw the elderly gentleman go crashing to the floor. The other blinked in surprise and exclaimed, "Harrup!" just before Harrup landed him a facer that sent him sprawling on top of his companion.

122

"Well done, Harrup!" she congratulated.

There was no answering smile, but only a black scowl. "Is that enough vulgarity for you?" he asked curtly.

She was not listening, but examining the bodies on the floor, which were showing signs of recovery. "They're all right. Let's get up to Cuthbert's place before someone else comes," she suggested.

Without answering, Harrup took her arm and drew her from the building.

"I don't see why you're in a pelter. You recognized one of the men, as we hoped to. Is he someone you and Markwell work with?"

"No, he is Lord Groden's second son," Harrup said through thin lips.

"Really! But how nice for you! You thought they were all as boring as Groden. There is one you'll have something in common with."

"I am not a drunkard, nor do I molest defenseless ladies," he said through thin lips.

Diana realized he was in no mood for conversation and went silently to the carriage. As soon as he had caught his breath, Harrup turned to revile her. "I must have been crazy, going along with your cork-brained idea!"

To avoid a lecture, she said, "We should hurry straight home. You might have received a threatening letter from Mrs. Whitby by now."

Harrup sighed wearily. "Of course I have. Nothing else would be a suitable finish for this night."

"Don't worry," Diana said, patting his hand. "Groden's son can't tell his papa you were there without revealing he was there, too."

"It's not Groden's son I'm worried about," he said in a hollow voice.

"Harrup! Who was the other man? If you tell me it was Lord Eldon—"

"Lord Eldon? No, it was no one so insignificant as the

lord chancellor. It was Prinney's brother, the Duke of York.''

"Oh!" A quick gasp of breath hung on the air. "How fortunate you already have the appointment. I daresay that could have hampered your getting it,'' she said, and held her breath to hear what he replied.

"I daresay it could," he answered, and closed his eyes. Diana was very much surprised that the next thing Harrup did was to begin laughing quite hysterically.

No letter had arrived when they reached Belgrave Square. Harrup had ceased his hysterics, and Diana tried to discover how serious his landing the Duke of York a facer might be.

"They no longer use the Tower of London as a holding pen for victims of the ax. I think that, like Groden's son, we may assume York won't want to broadcast his attendance at Laura's rout. As it's still early, we might as well begin planning *my* do. I want to have it before you and Peabody leave," he mentioned.

She was more than eager to change topics. "We should go home this week. You couldn't arrange a rout that quickly, could you?" she asked.

"Go home? You're not going to leave me before the Whitby business is finished?" he asked. He sounded shocked and even angry at the idea.

Something in her wanted to remain. She had become involved in the complications of his interesting life and would not be at all happy to leave before it was straightened out.

Regret soon turned to peevishness. "We can't stick around forever like a pair of barnacles," she answered gruffly. "Besides, it looks odd for me to be staying here with you. Lady Groden asked rather pointedly how long a visit I was making and whether I had any relatives in London. I know what she was getting at."

Harrup knew perfectly well the visit should end. There

was no impropriety in a short visit, particularly as Peabody was his cousin, but to lengthen it would raise a few questions. "Stay for the party, at least. We'll have it the day after tomorrow. That is an unexceptionable reason for remaining a little longer. Even Lady Groden realizes a party doesn't arrange itself. It requires a hostess—that is, someone to oversee the invitations and flowers and so on."

"Who usually does it for you?" she asked. "I know you frequently have parties."

"Mama, when she is in London. She is touring the Lake District with her sister this spring, however, which is why I require your help," he replied reasonably.

Diana considered this and agreed. "I do feel I ought to repay your kindness," she said. "I will be happy to write the invitations, but you must know I haven't a notion about ordering music or flowers or food for such a stylish do."

Mrs. Dunaway handles all that," he said, giving the lie to his mother's involvement in former parties.

"What does your mama do?"

"Nags."

Diana regarded him doubtfully. "I'll ask Lady Selena to help me," she decided, and looked closely for his reaction.

His first response was negative; then he suddenly changed his mind and said, "Excellent! And I shall try to spend a little more time at home, too—to get to know Selena better," he explained.

Harrup got the list of guests from his last party and went through it, deleting some names and adding others. "It will be just a small do," he said, handing her a sheet of paper bearing fifty names.

Diana blinked. "I am very happy it is to be so small. This will take hours. I'll ask Lady Selena to help me do the cards."

In the interest of haste, Mrs. Dunaway was apprised of the party that same evening and flew into a flurry of activity. Peabody offered her assistance. And Harrup, the cause

125

of it all, was left alone in his study, rubbing his chin and wondering if York had recognized him.

The next morning Diana was up early to discuss a few matters with Harrup before he left. She accompanied him to the door, still chattering. "I asked Ronald to drop around my office this morning," he mentioned. "I believe I've settled on the proper position for him, but I'll let him tell you himself."

Diana smiled warmly. "Thank you, Harrup," she said, and took his hand. Harrup squeezed her fingers tightly, and before he left, he lifted her hand to his lips and kissed it.

She mistrusted the sparkle in his eyes. "I hope you feel the same after you learn his post," he said, and left quickly.

Diana was on nettles, waiting to hear from Ronald. She wrote a note to Lady Selena requesting her help in arranging the party before she started writing the invitations. Lady Selena arrived so promptly, one would think she had been waiting with her pelisse and bonnet already on.

"It was kind of you to ask me to come." The lady smiled shyly. Looking all around the entrance hall, she added, "Is Ronald here?"

"No, he isn't," Diana replied. "The cards are in Harrup's office. Shall we begin writing them?" In the commotion, it hadn't occurred to her that Ronald and Selena would be thrown together. She would send Ronald off as soon as she learned his position.

He arrived within half an hour, smiling from ear to ear. "You'll never guess what, Di! I am to be Harrup's special assistant!" he crowed. Then his happy eyes fell on Lady Selena and glossed over in a surfeit of good fortune.

"Congratulations," Diana said, but already she foresaw considerable difficulty in this scheme. Although it was kind of Harrup to give Ronald such a good post, it seemed unwise in the face of Ronald's devotion to Lady Selena. This was why Harrup's eyes had been sparkling when he left.

Why had he done such a mischievous thing? She had warned him of the danger.

"Papa thought you were very clever last night," Lady Selena confided softly to Ronald.

"I would have been a deal more clever if I hadn't been trembling in my boots," he admitted.

"We are very happy for you, Ronald," Diana said. "And now, I'm afraid we must ask you to leave. Lady Selena and I have a hard morning's work before us."

"I am to help you," Ronald told her happily. "Harrup most particularly asked me to stay here today and give you any assistance I can for the party. It is my first assignment as his special assistant. Till he gets a desk and office fixed up for me, you know, I cannot do much at Westminster."

An angry buzzing sounded in Diana's ears. What was that wretched man up to? He knew Lady Selena would be here all day. He knew she would be too busy to ride herd on them as she ought to do. She lifted her chin and said coolly, "In that case, perhaps you should speak to Mrs. Dunaway and see what needs doing while Lady Selena and I write these cards."

"Oh, I'll help with the cards," Ronald said, and pulled a chair close to Selena's. "That is the first thing that needs doing. There is no point in arranging a party without guests. Why, Di, you haven't put RSVP on the bottom."

Mrs. Dunaway poked her head in the doorway and said, "The musicians are all booked up for tomorrow evening. I don't know what his lordship was about, thinking to throw together a scrambling do on such short notice. How can we have a rout without music?"

Ronald perked up his ears. "I might be able to round up a couple of fellows. Cuthbert's sister knows some chaps that fiddle for her parties. They're a new group just turning professional. They know all the new tunes, and I know where they practice."

"You'd best go after them," Diana decided.

Lady Selena bounced up from her chair. "I'll go with you, Ronald." She smiled.

"No, no! I need your help here, Selena," Diana said firmly.

Lady Selena looked abashed, but soon recovered. "I have the megrim, Miss Beecham. When I have the megrim, Mama always sends me out for a drive in the fresh air. I shall be back to help you very soon."

Diana stared helplessly while Ronald and Selena went off together, unchaperoned. She couldn't abandon her job, and even Peabody couldn't be spared to go with them. Someone had to help her write the cards.

"I am so annoyed with Harrup I could happily wring his neck," she complained to Peabody. "First giving Ronald the post as his special assistant, then sending him here to be underfoot with Selena all day."

Peabody stared. "You never mean he made our Ronald his special assistant, and you not telling me! Why, that is excellent news, Di. Aren't you happy for him?"

"Of course I am, but—oh, Peabody, it is too complicated. Here, you take this stack of cards. And don't forget to put RSVP on the bottom."

An hour passed, ninety minutes, and still Ronald and Selena did not return. What could possibly be taking them so long? Between worry and the rapid writing of the cards, Diana's head began to ache. As she finished the last card and added it to the stack, the front door opened and Ronald and Selena came in, laughing and talking happily.

Diana stormed into the hall, ready to rip at them. She looked at their smiling faces and felt like a jailer. They looked so right together, so happy—so much in love. "Did you manage to hire the musicians?" she asked in a tolerably patient voice.

"Yes, by Jove, and at an excellent price, too," Ronald assured her. "We had them play a few jigs for us so Selena

128

could judge whether their music was suitable. It's very easy to dance to. Of course Selena is so light-footed. . . ."

Diana fixed him with a sapient eye. "Is that how you construe your new duties, Ronald?" she asked coldly. "I didn't know you counted caper merchanting amongst your skills. Perhaps you would be kind enough to have these cards delivered." She handed him the stack. "And I don't mean for you to deliver them yourself. Give them to a footman."

The cards were just being piled into Ronald's arms when the door opened and Harrup entered. His eyes flew first to Diana's glowering face, from where they quickly flitted to Ronald and Selena. "All my helpers are hard at work, I see," he said heartily. Then he turned to Lady Selena and said, "Good morning, Selena. You are looking charming, as usual."

"Thank you," she said, but her face and expression were like thunder.

"May I see you for a moment in my office, Selena?" Harrup said. "There are a few things I wish to discuss about this evening."

Selena cast an imploring look to Ronald, who looked back helplessly as Harrup held the door for his fiancée. Selena entered with drooping shoulders and sullen lips. Diana was aware of a strong wish to put her ear to the keyhole and thought Ronald felt the same. Harrup obviously intended to try his hand at a spot of lovemaking. She had urged him to be kind to Selena and wondered why she should feel so incensed that he was taking her advice.

"You'd best get those cards delivered," she said to her brother. "In fact, you can deliver them yourself. Use Harrup's carriage." There was no danger of Selena accompanying him now.

"But Selena—" he said, looking to the closed door.

"Immediately," Diana added, and stared till Ronald walked away with the cards.

It was a quarter of an hour later when Selena came out of Harrup's office. She looked extremely unhappy. "Where is Ronald?" she asked Diana.

"He's gone. Is there something I can do for you?"

"No," the girl said sullenly.

Diana sought for words to discover what had passed in the office without sounding too encroaching. Obviously Harrup had used too heavy a hand in his lovemaking. "Is everything all right about this evening?" she ventured.

It was enough to set Selena off on a series of complaints. "He says I must stand in the welcome line with him and greet his guests. There will be cabinet ministers and possibly even the prime minister, Miss Beecham," she lamented. "And he has written this list with the title of each one, which I am supposed to memorize, and ask them questions or compliment them on their accomplishments."

Diana felt her head whirl. Was this his notion of conciliation? "Harrup and your parents will be with you, Selena," she pointed out. "You will not be expected to carry the whole burden yourself. You must be familiar with these gentlemen. I'm sure they have visited your house any number of times."

"They're all horrid." The girl pouted. "And I never can remember whether Castlereagh is the dandy little gentleman who flirts or the great fat one who looks like a hippopotamus. Harrup says it is very important that I not make any mistakes. It could jeopardize his career," she added, tears brimming in her eyes.

"You have the whole afternoon to learn the list," Diana said.

"I am going home, Miss Beecham. Pray tell Lord Harrup I have the megrim."

Lady Selena demanded her pelisse, and as her skirts whisked angrily out the door, Diana's whisked into Harrup's office. She cast a withering stare at Harrup, who looked back uneasily.

"I cannot believe you are such a flat," she began angrily. "Selena has just flounced off home with that list you gave her to memorize. Are you trying to frighten the life out of her?"

Harrup mounted his high horse and stared Diana down. "Not at all. My wife will have duties to perform. This is an excellent time for her to begin learning them."

"You can't expect her to learn the workings of government in one day, Harrup! And furthermore, what do you mean by making Ronald your special assistant, then sending him here when you knew I was asking Selena to help me?"

"I wanted to give you every assistance. It happens my office is in confusion at the moment, and I had no work for Ronald. I hope he proved useful to you?"

"Remarkably useful! He took Selena off to dance the morning away."

Harrup stared in bewilderment. "What?"

"Ronald undertook to hire musicians when Mrs. Dunaway could not engage your regular group. Selena went with him."

"I made sure the redoubtable Miss Beecham would keep a tight rein on the children for me," he mocked.

"I have no authority over the girl. I asked her to stay and help me. She said she had the megrim, and I might add she has it again. You may count yourself fortunate if she doesn't take to her bed with another this evening. I, for one, would scarcely blame her."

"Evils do come in threes, folks say," he agreed.

Diana felt better after venting her spleen and asked more mildly, "Speaking of evils, was there any mention from York about last night?"

"The *on-dit* at Whitehall is that the royal duke is at home with a bad cold, which had the curious effect of darkening his daylights."

131

"Then he's keeping mum," she interpreted. "Have you heard from Mrs. Whitby?"

"No." There was a sound of wheels on the street. Harrup strolled to the window. "Perhaps this is her note coming now."

Diana joined him, looking through the sheer curtain. "That's your own carriage. It must be Ronald delivering the cards." But she knew Ronald would be blocks away by now if he hadn't been hanging around, waiting for Selena. Even as she spoke, Lady Selena flew into the street and hurled herself into the carriage.

"Ronald will see her home safely," Harrup said.

"The devil he will. She'll be jaunting all over London with him, delivering those cards. You'll have to stop her."

Harrup looked serenely indifferent to this. "Did Ronald not assure you he meant to behave as a gentleman in this matter?"

"Yes, and to be fair, I think he will try, but that girl has no more notion of propriety than one of her own kittens. Ronald is not forceful enough to deny her anything."

He turned a black, accusing eye on her. "I can feel with Ronald in that predicament. How I ever let you talk me into going to Mrs. Whitby's!" Then he crossed his arms and considered the matter a moment. "I see no impropriety in my fiancée and my special assistant delivering invitations to my little rout. Even Groden would be hard pressed to discover any mischief there. The only person who might reasonably object is myself, and I have complete confidence in them both. Now shall we have some luncheon, Diana? I must return to work for a few hours this afternoon."

Her nostrils flared in indignation. "I am not at liberty, Harrup. Someone must arrange this demmed rout of yours, and it is clear that no one else will do it."

She stalked from the office and went to the ballroom to oversee the placement of vases for the flowers. The afternoon was taken up in discussions with Mrs. Dunaway and the servants regarding refreshments and other arrangements for the party.

Lady Selena did not return with Ronald, who arrived several hours later. "Is Harrup here?" were Ronald's first words, uttered with a telltale unsteadiness of the eyes that spoke of guilt.

"No. Where's Selena?"

"I left her at home. It is unconscionable the way that man treats her, Di."

"Standing at the door and welcoming his guests is hardly a punishment," she defended.

"No, but the way he spoke to her—so harshly. Telling her she must read up on politics and not make a cake of herself by appearing ignorant of what passes in the world. She said he reminded her of her papa, talking nothing but politics. He told her the attorney general's wife must circulate and play the hostess, putting his guests at their ease. His lady, he said, was not expected to sit on the sofa like a cushion, as she did the other night at Groden's dinner party. You know how shy Selena is, Di. It will be torture for her. If I didn't know better, I would think Harrup was trying to give her a disgust of him."

"Nonsense, he is only showing her how she must behave after they are married."

Ronald stood irresolute a moment; then he straightened his narrow shoulders and spoke firmly. "There is such a thing as pushing people too far. 'My foe may provide me with arms.' That is all I have to say."

"Might I suggest you say it to Harrup?" she replied. "There is no point in complaining to me, Ronald. I don't rule the roost here."

Ronald's courage did not go quite that far. He was going to Whitehall to see if his office was ready yet, but Diana knew he wouldn't speak to his patron on personal matters. It wasn't Ronald's style.

The newspapers had several stories on Harrup's appointment, some of them giving a detailed history of the family. Peabody brought the papers to Diana, as proud as though Chuggie were her own son. "I always knew Chuggie would amount to something." She smiled dotingly. "Such a clever boy as he was. We will see him prime minister yet, Di. Mark my words. And he'll carry our Ronald along with him to the top. You may have your wish of lording it over them all in London yet."

"I never wanted to lord it over anyone. Only to be allowed to hang on the fringes and watch the great at work and play. I begin to feel even that is overestimated."

Harrup was out that evening. He didn't dine at home or tell Diana where he was going, but she learned from Mrs. Dunaway that some of his colleagues were having a party at one of the clubs to celebrate his promotion, which meant that Lady Selena would not be with him. Perhaps the young lady would spend her free time memorizing her list. Diana felt sorry for the girl and for Ronald, but mostly she was angry with Harrup.

He had promised he would ingratiate Selena. She felt he could do it, too, if only he would put himself to the bother. Why did he not? It looked as though he meant to continue his libertine ways after marriage and didn't want a wife who clung too closely to him. Perhaps he had even hired Ronald to give Selena a convenient young cicisbeo, someone to amuse her while he amused himself with the muslin company?

This interpretation explained a series of otherwise inexplicable decisions on Harrup's part—hiring Ronald, encouraging proximity between him and Selena, and doing nothing to make his future bride like him. It was a disgusting, cynical way to behave, especially with such innocents as Selena and Ron, but no other explanation could she find.

Diana had some intention of accosting him when he came

134

in and taking him to task, but his party lasted very late. She was sound asleep when Harrup returned, slightly bosky, and looked hopefully into his office to see if she was there.

Chapter Nine

After his late night, Harrup did not reach the breakfast table till nine the next morning. Diana was already in hand with the rout arrangements. It was in the ballroom that he found her later, overseeing the placement of some bent-wood chairs to hold the dowagers while the younger members of the party danced. Purple smudges shadowed the area beneath Harrup's eyes. The eyes themselves showed signs of ravage from his late-night revels. With these traces of dissipation on him, Diana found it easy to believe him capable of her worst imaginings.

She regarded him with distaste. "Good morning, Harrup. No need to ask if you slept well. You look like a roué."

Harrup sensed that he was in poor aroma and answered carefully. "It's not every evening a man celebrates a major triumph. I confess, the wine flowed freely. Did anything interesting happen here?"

She glared at him mutinously. "Nothing that would interest you," she said curtly.

"What happens under my roof always interests me. I sense this discussion requires privacy," he added, when a few servants began listening in. "Shall we go to my office?"

Diana was undecided whether to oblige him or not, but

her anger was choking her, and she went. Harrup carefully closed the door before turning to her. "Let's hear it," he said. "Your eyes aren't burning like flame for no reason. What has my new assistant been up to?"

"Your assistant, unfortunately, hasn't the backbone to rake your hair with a stool as he ought to. I, being Ronald's elder sister, shall undertake to do it for him. I am not at all happy with the situation you've created here, Harrup, and I don't mean to return home without rectifying it."

"Situation?" he asked, blinking.

She stared scornfully at his face, which was pale from drinking and from his late night. "The situation of your making Ronald your assistant, whose major chore appears to be entertaining your bride-to-be. I have warned you before of the attachment between them. Unlike Peabody, I don't believe it was any desire to oblige old neighbors that led you to honor Ronald. I thought at first it was only mischief, but I begin to see a more sinister plan."

"Indeed? Perhaps you would care to enlighten me as to the nature of this sinister design?" he asked stiffly.

"I cannot think it necessary, but I *will* tell you what I think, because if I don't tell someone, I shall scream. I think you hired Ronald to provide a convenient escort for your bride, thus leaving you free to continue your wanton ways with such females as Mrs. Whitby. If that is how you intend to proceed as a married man, I must insist you choose another dupe than my innocent young brother. How your conscious can allow you to play off such a stunt on Selena passes my comprehension, but then, I have not had the advantage of a career in the asylum of politics, where apparently anything goes. Fifteen years now you've been on the town. I should think that would be enough to give even you your fill of debauchery."

Harrup listened in rigid silence. She expected every moment that he would attack. He looked tense, ready to spring at her throat, but he said nothing till she had finished.

137

"Thank you for that edifying reading of my character," he said coldly. "I am sorry to have caused you concern. You will be pleased to know that even I, steeped in lechery as I am, do not enter into marriage with any intention of offering my bride's favors to the first pup who comes sniffing around. Fifteen years of dissipation has indeed proven sufficient for me. Like most ladies, you overrate the attraction of your sex. My career is more important to me now, and after the Whitby affair, I see the two do not mix."

"Then why do you not forbid Ronald to dangle after Selena?" she demanded.

"Forbidden fruit is always sweeter. My long experience in ruining women has taught me that much at least. Let 'em have their fill of rolling their eyes at each other. It won't go further than that, I promise you."

Diana listened but was still not satisfied. "You're doing everything in your power to turn Selena against you. Writing her that list, and telling her she must suddenly be an accomplished political hostess, when she doesn't even know the prime minister's name."

"High time she learned," he snapped. "My wife will have strenuous social duties. If Lady Selena is incapable of fulfilling them, then the time to learn it is before the wedding, not after."

"No, Harrup, the time to learn was before the betrothal. The fact of the matter is, you snatched at Groden's offer because Selena is pretty, wellborn, and well dowered, and you thought you'd have a better chance at the coveted promotion if you had a wife. That she is a peagoose who holds you in the greatest aversion didn't matter a groat. Now that you realize the inconvenience of a child bride, you have decided to turn her into something she is not and never will be. I wish you luck of your bargain, but pray leave Ronald out of it."

Harrup narrowed his eyes in a frown. "Are you asking me to dismiss him?"

138

"No! Change the nature of his duties. Even a greenhead like Ronald can be pushed too far. Put him behind a desk and give him some real work to do, instead of encouraging him to taggle at her apron strings. You shouldn't have sent him here yesterday when you knew Selena would be here. You owe me that much," she added, and held his eyes with an imperious blaze from her own.

"Perhaps you're right," he admitted mildly.

"You know I'm right. Will you do it, Harrup? Will you promise to keep him busy and out of mischief with Selena? It is to your own advantage to do it. Don't expect him to share your sophisticated mores regarding women. He won't try to seduce her behind your back, you know. He'll convince her to divorce you, and you may imagine what that would do to your career."

"I notice you couch your urgings in a manner to appeal to my self-interest. That is hardly flattering, Diana."

"I do you the honor of saying precisely what is in my mind, milord."

"No, madam, you try to manipulate me. What you actually fear is that Ronald will make a flaming jackass of himself and be booted out on his ear. You don't give a tinker's curse about my career or my reputation."

"Didn't I rescue your letters from Markwell?" she reminded him.

"Did you not do it to have a club to hold over my head so I'd be obliged to find your brother a job?"

"That was only part of the reason. I also disliked to see disgrace come into our parish, and to see your mother suffer."

"Your benevolence extends to everyone except myself, in fact."

"You didn't need my benevolence. You've been cock of the walk for so long, you don't need anyone. If Whitby becomes a problem, you'll pour money into her purse. Slice a libertine where you will, he's a libertine all the way through. You'll buy whatever you need or want. Too much money, and too much consequence—I expect that's what has made you the way you are," she added, with a derisive sneer.

"Kind of you to find an excuse for the inexcusable. Is there anything else you wish to say to me? If not, this walking pattern of sin and corruption has some duties to attend to."

She made a mock curtsy. "I would not wish to detain the nation's chief law officer. By all means, you must write up some taboos for the mere mortals of the land. We must be careful to do as you decree and not as you do."

Harrup observed her for a moment before leaving. The lines etched from nose to lips gave him a satirical appearance that was not lessened by the glint in his eyes. "Did you always hate me," he asked, "or is it only familiarity that has bred this contempt?"

"To tell the truth, I scarcely thought about you at all. It wasn't till I had an opportunity to see you at close range that I realized your deficiencies."

A flush suffused his lean cheeks. "It would be ungentlemanly for me to say that cuts two ways. And incidentally, Miss Beecham, you might be interested to know I spoke to Ronald yesterday afternoon about his outing with Lady Selena. I warned him away from too much familiarity—I told him *some* people would be small-minded enough to discern harm in it. Ronald agreed with me that we would not wish to cast any aspersions on the future Lady Harrup. He is busy at his desk this morning and will spend the day there."

Although Diana was relieved to hear it, she resented that Harrup hadn't told her before she flew into her unnecessary rage. "You might have told me before—"

"Before you made a gudgeon of yourself?" he asked, smiling through thin lips. "If I had interrupted your tirade, I would never have learned what you really think of me.

Good day.'' He bowed ceremoniously and strode toward the door.

"Harrup, wait!''

He turned slowly and looked at her. Was it possible that glint in his eyes was amusement? If so, it ran his anger a close race. "I—I'm sorry,'' she said brusquely. "I misunderstood. I didn't mean to plunge myself into your affairs.''

He hunched his shoulders. "Plunge away. You weren't totally wrong in your assessment of my character. You merely forgot that *I* have a brain, too. When a man reaches my age, he begins to take an accounting of his past life. I was not quite so harsh on myself as you were, but our conclusions ran in the same groove. Where we diverge is in your believing me beyond redemption. Friends?'' he asked, lifting a brow.

She nodded reluctantly. "Friends,'' she agreed.

But it was an uneasy parting. She felt she had said more than was necessary and lost Harrup's goodwill into the bargain. Harrup went to get his coat, and Diana remained behind in his office, thinking, mostly regretting her outburst. She should have known Harrup wasn't that bad. He wasn't a fool, at least. Pride, if nothing else, would make him straighten Ronald out. To distract her mind from these worries, she thought of the party. Now what needed doing? She could oversee the setting of the tables.

She went into the hall just as the door knocker sounded. She feared it was Lady Selena, but with Ronald absent, the young lady would not remain long. Stoker opened the door and a lady's genteel accent was heard. Diana recognized Mrs. Whitby's voice and gasped audibly, her eyes flying to Harrup, who was putting on his coat. Mrs. Whitby looked very beautiful in a violet pelisse with mink collar, on which rested a dainty bouquet of violets. An impressive bonnet composed of feathers and flowers sat on her raven head, and in her hands she carried a mink muff. Her bright blue eyes toured the hall, spotting Diana and roving on till they espied Harrup in the corner.

"Mrs. Whitby to see you, milord," Stoker announced with a disapproving stare.

"Good morning, Charles," the woman said, and walked in, her hips swinging insouciantly. "I expect you know why I am here." With a mocking smile she added, "I have come to offer my congratulations on your appointment."

"Good morning, Laura," Harrup replied woodenly. "Nice to see you again."

He smiled numbly and showed her to his office. Over his shoulder he looked a plea at Diana, beckoning to her with a toss of his head to follow them. She was surprised, but not at all loath to accept, and hastened after them.

Mrs. Whitby turned in surprise. "Miss Beecham, isn't it?" she asked politely, as though this were a normal morning call.

"Yes," Diana answered. Her voice sounded strangely high.

They all sat down. Harrup looked expectantly at his caller, who smoothed her skirt and glanced around at the office. "Very nice, Charles. I believe this is the first time I've been here."

"And, I trust, the last," he answered blandly. "Why have you waited so long, Laura?"

"I don't believe you ever invited me to your home before."

"I didn't invite you today. I referred to your delay in coming to dun me."

She smiled demurely. "Timing is so important, don't you think? Two days ago a minister without portfolio called on me with a little pourboire of five hundred pounds to buy my silence. That bought two days, Charles. Today the attorney general will be more generous, I think. Rather like the stock market. Your stock has risen, dear boy. Now is the time to sell out."

"Then you kept the letters?" Harrup asked.

"I could not bear to part with those special two," she taunted. "You *do* remember the gist of them, Charles? Perhaps not. Truth to tell, I feared you were disguised when you penned them—such an uncharacteristic warmth from the discreet privy councillor. You have no idea how precious they had become to me. You must know after quizzing my woman how close the billets-doux are to my heart." She smiled fondly.

Diana figured this farce has gone on long enough and looked a question at Harrup. "She has them on her. This is our chance," she said.

Mrs. Whitby laughed benignly. "She is precious, Charles. Wherever did you find this original? One of your milkmaids, *peut-être?*"

Harrup just looked, his gaze centering on the caller's bodice. "I didn't bring them with me," Mrs. Whitby told him. "No, no, I transferred them to a safe-deposit box after my woman told you their usual hiding place. I know you're busy, Charles, especially with your dear little bride and her family to be entertained this evening. My, wouldn't Lord Groden open up his eyes to see the letters. All the Westminster worthies will be assembling there, Markwell tells me."

"You are back under Markwell's protection now, are you, Laura?" Harrup asked.

Looking at him, Diana found it hard to believe he was as angry as he should be. He had looked worse when she was railing at him herself a moment earlier. Why didn't he try to discover where this safe-deposit box was located?

"It has come to that, in the end," Mrs. Whitby admitted. "I was a little vexed with him for stealing your letters. He didn't tell me what he was up to, the sly rogue. But I daresay I shall keep him in line." A bold, mocking smile did much to destroy the woman's beauty.

Diana saw a trace of how Mrs. Whitby would look in

ten years—avaricious, petty, mean. "So, shall we discuss terms?" the hussy asked.

"The terms are that you may take the infamous letters to Lord Groden with my blessing, madam. He'll have you tossed into the gutter."

Mrs. Whitby made a *tsk*ing sound. "Really, Charles! I am not a savage. I would not dream of interfering with your very profitable marriage. You'll need the child's dowry to pay me. I merely meant to sell the letters to one of the lesser newspapers. Markwell suggested a Whig rag might be more generous—the *Morning Chronicle*, perhaps." She preened her hair and smiled brightly.

"What price did Markwell suggest you might gouge out of me?" Harrup asked.

"Five thousand. I swear the boy is still wet behind the ears." She laughed gaily. "My friends tell me Lady Selena brings you twenty. I'll have half. Cash will do fine. You can bring it to me this afternoon. That will leave you a few hours to arrange it with your banker."

Diana looked from one to the other, wondering what Harrup would do. He had never mentioned such a high sum as ten thousand. Surely he would not comply, but she saw only frustration blazing in his eyes and an effort not to show Mrs. Whitby how angry he was. How could they discover which bank the safe-deposit box was at? Surely the attorney general could gain access to it.

"I wouldn't want to throw you to the cent percenters," Mrs. Whitby continued. "If I catch you a trifle short, I'm sure the banks will be happy to oblige Lady Selena's fiancé and the attorney general."

It struck Diana that the attorney general ought to be able to clamp this wretched woman into chains. Surely blackmail was against the law. There must be something a man in Harrup's position could do.

She assumed a bold face and said, "You are brave, coming to threaten the attorney general in his own home, Mrs.

144

Whitby. I fear you aren't completely aware of the prerogatives he now enjoys.'' She shot a meaningful look at Harrup, trying to convey that he should invent some awful threat. She could see he was thinking wildly, but nothing came from his lips.

Left to her own devices, Diana pulled a solution, or at least a delaying tactic, out of the air. She gazed innocently at Mrs. Whitby. ''Were you not aware that the attorney general has access to *all* safe-deposit boxes in the city? So kind of you to tell us where you keep the letters.'' She turned to speak to Harrup next. ''You really ought to run along to Whitehall, Charles,'' using his name for no other reason but to show Mrs. Whitby she was on an intimate footing with Harrup, too. ''You will want to put a great many men on this matter. You won't have time to go to seize all the boxes yourself.''

Harrup nodded thoughtfully. ''I believe the better way would be to send word to all the trust company and bank managers and inquire from them which one enjoys Mrs. Whitby's business. Unless you'd care to save me the bother and tell me yourself, Laura?'' he asked politely.

Mrs. Whitby proved indomitable under attack. She smiled blandly. ''I don't believe the attorney general enjoys any such privilege,'' she answered.

Diana tossed her a challenging stare. ''Don't you, Mrs. Whitby? But it's a dangerous chance to take, is it not?''

Mrs. Whitby began to stir restively in her seat. She tried to keep up a firm facade, but there were chinks of uncertainty appearing in her armor. She rose rather hastily and said, ''I shall look for you around three, Charles—with my little pourboire. *Au revoir.* Nice to have met you again, Miss Beecham.''

''Enchantée,'' Diana answered ironically.

The woman swept from the room, and Harrup stared at Diana. ''I don't have access to any safe-deposit boxes!'' he said.

145

"*She* doesn't know that. And she won't dare to take the chance. She'll dart straight off to her bank and collect the letters."

"She's not that stupid."

"I tell you she'll do it! We must go after her. Charles, write up something official-looking and stamp a big red seal on it. We'll follow her, and when she goes to her box, you speak to the manager and insist he give you the contents. Say it's—say it's letters from a spy," she advised.

Harrup just stared in wonder. "You're insane! I can't do that!"

"Yes, you can. You're the attorney general."

"That is precisely why I can't do it! Noblesse oblige. My duty is to uphold the law, not mutilate it. I, of all people, cannot use coercion. It would ruin me if it got out, and you may be sure that with Markwell for her mentor, Whitby wouldn't be long in making a public scandal of it."

Diana glared. "I never thought you were so lily livered!" she snipped, and stormed from the room.

"Stoker, call the carriage at once!" she shouted as she hastened forward.

"What's afoot, miss?" he asked cheerfully. "If you're going after the lightskirt, you'd best take his lordship's curricle. It was brought round ten minutes ago."

"Stoker, you were eavesdropping!" she exclaimed, and laughed in excitement.

He handed her her bonnet and pelisse and helped her into them. "You was all talking a bit loud, miss."

He held the door wide, and Diana dashed out. Mrs. Whitby's carriage was just turning the corner, heading toward Piccadilly. Harrup's tiger sat on the perch of his master's dashing yellow curricle. "Move over, and follow that rig!" Diana ordered.

The tiger sat still, just looking over her shoulder. "Hurry up!" she ordered.

"I'll take the ribbons, Podey," Harrup said. He had rushed out after Diana. The tiger hopped down, and Harrup took the driver's seat.

"Spring 'em," Diana said eagerly. "She's going north. She might be going to the bank or home. Did you get a seal onto a piece of paper?" She knew Harrup was a first-rate fiddler, and was happy to see that he didn't hesitate to use the whip.

"No, but I'll follow her at a discreet distance and just see where she goes."

"If she takes the letters out of her safe-deposit box, we'll have a chance at them," Diana said, thinking aloud.

"And if she doesn't?" he asked.

"As long as they're in a vault, they can't do much damage. We mustn't let her out of our sight. There, she's turning east on Piccadilly."

Mrs. Whitby's black carriage didn't waste a minute. Harrup's grays were driven hard to keep up with it. "You shouldn't have bought her such good nags," Diana scolded.

"I'll bear that in mind—in the unlikely event that I ever purchase nags for another woman!" he added hastily.

"I hope this has taught you a lesson! Oh, look, Harrup! She's going to New Bond Street. I made sure she would go home and dash a note off to Markwell, but she didn't turn off at Glasshouse. Surely she's not going shopping!"

Mrs. Whitby alighted from her carriage and, with a footman to lend her dignity, began a tour of the shops. "She's going to see your curricle. We'll have to get down and walk," Diana said.

Harrup drew in at a curb behind a large carriage for concealment and pulled out his watch. "I am now eighteen minutes late for a cabinet meeting. That will make a fine impression—my first meeting as attorney general and I'm late."

"You'll have to go on, then," Diana decided.

"I can't leave you downtown alone."

"Oh, really, Harrup! I'm not a child. There, she's gone into a drapery store. She might be there forever." Without further ado, Diana hopped down from the perch and began pacing toward the drapery store. Harrup was not two steps behind her.

"Diana, get back in the carriage. I'll take you home."

"Go on to Whitehall. Oh, Harrup, perhaps you'd best give me some money in case I have to follow her in a cab."

"I can't leave you here alone," he repeated.

"Send Ronald down to bear me company. Oh, and let him bring the curricle in case we have to follow Mrs. Whitby's carriage."

Harrup's eyes widened in astonishment. "Let that cawker drive my grays! He could cripple a Clydesdale."

"Idiot!" She laughed, her eyes dancing with excitement. "I'll drive them once he gets here. I am an excellent whip. Now go on, before Lord Liverpool is angry with you."

"You couldn't begin to control this team. This is ridiculous! I'll pay Whitby the money. Get in the carriage, Diana."

She held her hand out impatiently. "I'll need about ten guineas."

"Cabs don't cost that much!"

"No, skint, but I've had an idea. I'm going to buy a new bonnet and pelisse so she won't recognize me if she happens to look over her shoulder. She's seen this outfit, and unless she's blind as a bat, she knows we're following her. If the curricle is gone when she comes out—well, perhaps she'll think you've given up, and then she'll nip in to her bank and get the letters."

"What good will that do?"

"We'll *know,* and can make new plans," she explained. "Oh, really, Harrup, I expected better of you. You're no more help than Ronald. Please go on!" she urged, pushing

148

him toward his carriage. "The sooner you get to your office, the sooner Ronald can come and help me. The money," she said again, holding out her hand. Harrup, between frustration, hope, and despair, handed her his purse and hopped into the curricle. He gave a worried look over his shoulder as he left and nearly sideswiped a passing gig.

The last thing he saw was Diana shaking her head at him in disbelief as such poor fiddling. A reluctant smile tugged at his lips as he whipped up the team and darted to Whitehall.

Once she was alone, Diana opened Harrup's purse and stared at a thick wad of bills. She watched the drapery shop, and as there was no sign of Mrs. Whitby emerging yet, she went into the millinery shop across the street. Stationing herself at the window to watch her quarry, she asked the saleswoman to bring her the hat that was most unlike the one she wore.

With a look at the rather plain navy blue bonnet the young lady had on, the clerk gave her a red straw that suited her notions of what a hussy who dunned her beau for money on the street and went shopping alone would like. It was a high poke bonnet trimmed with white gardenias.

Without even trying it on, Diana said, "I'll take it. Please put my old one in a box. That might be useful." She could hold the box in front of her face if Mrs. Whitby looked at her too closely.

"I need a new pelisse, too," Diana said.

"This is a millinery shop, ma'am. We do not sell pelisses."

Diana kept looking out the window, speaking over her shoulder. "I must have one. What color is yours, ma'am?"

"It is green, madam, and it is not for sale."

"I'll give you five pounds for it," Diana said.

"But, madam, you haven't even seen it."

"Hurry up! She's leaving."

Five pounds for a pelisse worth two was too good a bargain to miss. The clerk darted to the rear of the shop and placed a green pelisse over the blue pelisse on this deranged young lady's shoulders. It clashed horridly with the red bonnet. Diana shoved the money at her, grabbed the hat box, and ran from the store, looking much worse than when she had entered but certainly very different. When the sales clerk saw her crouch behind the parked carriage in front of her shop, she gave serious consideration to sending off for a Bow Street Runner.

Mrs. Whitby stood on the street, looking carefully up and down. She had seen Harrup's curricle leave, and knew he had been alone. Surely Miss Beecham had no authority to seize her letters? She suspected Miss Beecham was loitering about to follow her and began a leisurely stroll up New Bond Street, stopping at every window for a surreptitious peek around. An occasional glimmer of red and green was seen across the street, but it didn't seem suspicious. She knew Miss Beecham had been wearing something dark. Only a lower member of of the muslin company would be seen in bright red and green. Some country chit just arrived in town, she assumed. But when the red bonnet was still across the street two blocks later, she stepped up her lookout.

Diana jumped into the first passing cab and changed her bonnet. The cab driver was ordered to park, and when he objected to this, he was given two pound notes, for which he would gladly have parked in the middle of St. James's Palace. When Mrs. Whitby walked on, the driver was told to follow her, drawing to a stop within sight of her. While this game of cat and mouse was going forth, Lord Harrup's curricle went bucketing past, very inexpertly driven by Ronald.

Diana opened the window and shouted at him before he reached Mrs. Whitby. He stopped, and she clambered up beside him. "Thank heavens you got here. You'll have to park this rig, Ronald. Mrs. Whitby will recognize it."

"Di, what the devil is going on? I think Harrup has had a knock on the head. He told me to drive his grays down to New Bond Street and look for you. How did he know you were here, and what are you doing—alone? And most of all, why is he making me drive this wild team?" he complained, jobbing at their sensitive mouths.

Ronald found a boy to hold the reins, and before he knew what was going on, Diana had him following Mrs. Whitby, dodging behind other pedestrians to keep out of sight. She explained the situation to him as best she could. "So that is why we cannot lose sight of her."

"This sounds like one of your harebrained schemes. And what do we do when she gets her letters from the bank?" he asked.

"We follow her and try to get them back, of course. Actually I begin to think it was all a hum. She cannot think I'm still following her. I'm sure she hasn't seen me for an age. She doesn't have the letters in a safe-deposit box at all."

Ronald looked down and smiled. "I think she does, Di. She just turned in at the New England Bank."

Chapter Ten

Diana passed for a notable whip in the sparsely populated county where she lived. She hopped onto the perch with no qualms on that score. She managed to walk Harrup's grays half a block with no difficulty, though she was somewhat nervous at the quantity and proximity of other carriages and their drivers' way of assuming she would make room for them all. Even the gentlemen drivers didn't move over an inch but seemed to take some perverse pleasure in squeaking past a female whipster and frightening her.

She had to whip the team to a trot when Mrs. Whitby's carriage drove past the busy area and stepped up its pace. A pair of prime bloods that hadn't been exercised much that day were soon jolting along at a breakneck pace that no amount of jobbing on the reins could decrease. Yet despite Diana's dangerous speed, Mrs. Whitby's carriage was pulling away from her. Carriages and pedestrians and shops whizzed past at a dizzying speed that set Diana's head whirling.

"Ronald," she said faintly, "I think you should take the reins. My arms are becoming tired."

Ronald looked fearfully at the galloping nags, their manes and tales blowing in the wind. He looked at the carriages flying past at what looked like a hundred miles an hour and said diffidently, "I'll take one. Between us, we'll manage."

She was too distraught to find any humor in this ludicrous suggestion. "They're a team, sapskull!" She scowled, knowing there was to be no help from that source.

Mrs. Whitby's carriage turned sharp left onto Glasshouse Street. "She's nearly home," Diana fretted. "Once she gets those letters into her house, we're lost. There would be hundreds of places to hide them. We've got to stop her."

"What you've got to stop is these wild prads," Ronald squealed as she executed a wobbly turn that required the strenuous use of both hands to allow him to remain seated.

Mrs. Whitby's carriage had begun to slow down as she approached home. Diana didn't realize it till she was around the corner and found herself only a few yards behind the black carriage. Her fingers ached from the effort of making the horses turn the corner. She eased them off the reins for a moment, and Harrup's team took the notion they were free to bolt. Before she could blink, they charged to the side of Mrs. Whitby's carriage, obviously intending to pass it. For a moment, the two rigs ran side by side.

Diana glanced down and saw Mrs. Whitby's angry, frightened face glaring up at her from the window. Her jaw was clenched in determination, and she looked ugly. In that fleeting second she noticed the rosy cheeks had blanched to white, with a circle of pink rouge riding unnaturally in the center. The next things she noticed were the whinnying of frightened horses, the earsplitting oaths of Mrs. Whitby's groom, and the sickening sound of breaking wood. Mrs. Whitby's horses had reared in fright, sending Harrup's grays into pandemonium. Their instinct was to bolt faster, but with the curricle wheels enmeshed in those of the carriage, not even that pair of bloods could proceed.

The curricle, being the lighter vehicle, tipped over, its fall to the ground impeded by the black carriage. Diana wrenched her shoulder and lost her bonnet in the fall, but remained conscious throughout. When she determined that she could move and that Ronald was only wounded, she looked at Mrs. Whitby. Through the shattered glass she saw the woman sprawled against the squabs of her elegant chaise, her lovely bonnet knocked askew as she slowly sank to the floor with her eyes closed.

Without a moment's hesitation, Diana flew around and clambered in at the other door. She found Mrs. Whitby's reticule on the seat beside her, but the letters were not in it. She carefully unbuttoned the woman's jacket and felt in her bodice—again nothing. Where were the letters? She tried the pockets of the chaise and found only a small flask of brandy. Then her eyes alighted on the mink muff on the floor—a fairly large muff. She thrust her fingers inside and felt the satisfying outline of two envelopes. She tried to extract them, but they were wedged in tightly. Without a moment's hesitation she took the muff and began to climb out of the carriage.

Mrs. Whitby regained consciousness in time to yell "Stop! Thief!"

The footman grabbed Diana's arm and whirled her around. Diana tossed the muff to Ronald, who was just climbing up from the rubble.

During the ensuing brouhaha, the groom ran off for a Bow Street Runner, the footman held Diana tightly by the arm, Mrs. Whitby had recourse to the brandy and began to raise a mighty racket, Ronald discovered the letters in the muff and secreted them in his own pocket and came to his sister's aid.

"Where are they?" Diana whispered. He patted his pocket. "We're going to be arrested. You'd better hide them."

"Where?" he asked.

"Put them under the seat of Harrup's curricle. Pretend

154

you're seeing to the horses. In fact, Ronald, *do* see to the horses. If they're harmed, Harrup will kill us."

As the footman couldn't hold two lively youngsters prisoner at one time, Ronald did as he was told. He also brought the red bonnet and put it on Diana's head. "You don't want to go to Bow Street without a bonnet. You'd look like a hoyden," he said.

Mrs. Whitby had searched the carriage and discovered her missing muff. She began railing at Diana, accusing her of stealing it.

"Why, there it is on the road," Diana pointed out. "It must have gotten thrown from the carriage during the accident."

Mrs. Whitby ran to retrieve it. She put her hands inside and leveled an accusing stare at Miss Beecham. "You'll go to Bridewell for this, my girl. Give me those letters, or I swear I'll turn you over to the authorities."

"What letters, ma'am?" Diana asked, and refused to budge from that position.

The Bow Street Runner soon arrived, eager to do his duty. He was in little doubt as to who was the guilty party. A top-of-the-trees lady like Mrs. Whitby, reeking of respectability, was obviously the victim of this garish hussy who looked like a character in a Christmas masque.

Harrup's prime bits of blood and Ronald's simple elegance pegged him as the lightskirt's gent. "Is this your lady, sir?" the runner asked Ronald, with a jab of his finger toward Diana.

"Certainly not! She's my sister," Ronald answered.

"Oh, lawks, that is sweet of you, lad." Diana smirked and set her red bonnet at a saucy angle. "I wouldn't want to get a nice boy like yourself into no trouble. You just run along and tend to your nags—and the carriage," she added, fixing him with a commanding stare. "I'm sure you have some business to attend to. No need to sully your character by appearing in court. I can take care of myself. And thanks for the ride, mister.''

"Run along, lad, and let it be a lesson to you," the Runner said kindly. "You don't want to associate with such saucy articles as this female. You'll only end up in the suds. But you'd best leave your name and address."

Diana nodded vigorously, and Ronald, though loath to abandon her, figured his first duty was to save his patron's reputation and did as the Runner suggested. George Cuthbert's name was taken in vain again.

"I want this woman stripped and searched," Mrs. Whitby decreed. "She has stolen something that belongs to me."

"What would that be, miss?" Diana asked boldly.

"We both know what I am talking about."

The Runner hauled Diana down to Bow Street, with Mrs. Whitby bringing up the rear. Diana gabbled all the way, using such stable expressions as had come her way. "I swear the gentry mort's talking through her hat," she said. "I didn't steal nothing." Lord Harrup occurred to her as a possible character reference, only to be dismissed. She had plenty of his money with her, and when Ronald returned, he must attend to the technicalities. Her only fear was that Ronald would not return.

The search was every bit as demeaning as she feared it would be, but at least a woman was given the chore of overseeing it. Diana stripped down to her petticoat and allowed the female to examine her.

"Clean as a whistle," the searcher proclaimed. "But you still have to account for that wad of blunt in your reticule, Miss Peabody."

Diana winced to remember what name had popped into her head when a name was asked for. She had to forgive Ronald for using his friend's names as an alias. "I earned it by the sweat of my brow," Diana said nonchalantly. "A fine gent give it to me last night. All I had to do was—"

The woman stared at her. "And he bought me this dandy bonnet and cape this morning, too," she added.

"Very elegant, I'm sure," the searcher said.

Mrs. Whitby had not accused the female of stealing money. "Some papers," she had said, and there were no valuable papers in the young female's reticule other than the cash.

"So what happens to me now?" Diana inquired.

"That depends on what charges Mrs. Whitby decides to lay. It will be for your young gentleman to settle up for her smashed carriage. I don't fancy he let you take the ribbons," she added.

"Oh, lud, is that what all the commotion is about? I'll pay for her carriage."

"You can wait in the room with the other women," the searcher said, and led Diana to a small, dirty, windowless room inhabited by a few female cutpurses and prostitutes and two drunken old hags whose sins remained a mystery, for they were sound asleep. Diana went and sat on a chair in the corner to isolate herself from the human misery around her. She felt compassion for the unfortunate women, but no desire to associate with them. Their talk was loud and lewd, punctuated by much laughter, but she sensed the desperation beneath their carefree facades.

While Diana was being put through her paces, Ronald went to examine Harrup's team and carriage. He saw at a glance that the only possible salvage from the curricle was one wheel, which hardly seemed worth the bother. The nags pawed the ground restively. A close examination of their legs showed they had escaped damage. It was only their mouths that were a trifle the worse for wear. He retrieved the important letters from beneath the seat. His eye fell on Diana's navy bonnet, and he thought he ought to take it along for safekeeping. He picked it up and led the team to the closest livery stable.

"There's a dandy curricle all smashed to bits on Glasshouse Street, just off Bond. You can have what's left if you'll haul it away," he explained.

This was acceptable to the owner, who agreed to handle it and stable Harrup's bloods till they were called for.

Ronald deemed rescuing Diana more important than getting the letters to Harrup. His patron was at a meeting that would continue past noon in any case, and he disliked to interrupt him there. With a host of doubts that he was doing the right thing, he turned his steps to Bow Street and did battle with the authorities.

It was two hours before a carriage maker came up with an estimate of damage to the Whitby carriage. Two hundred pounds seemed inordinately high, but as Diana had the money, they paid it. Ronald got off with a warning, and as no stolen property was discovered on Diana, she was allowed to go free, too. Mrs. Whitby was in high dudgeon at the inefficacy of the law, but she knew she had been bested, and left without further trouble. With a sorry look at her sister inhabitants of the small back room, Diana handed the red bonnet and green cape to the shabbiest of them and put on her own clothes.

"Where are the letters?" were her first words when she and Ronald breathed free air outside the detention house.

Ronald handed them to her. Diana gazed at them, two little pieces of paper appearing totally innocent, but they had nearly cost her her reputation and Harrup ten thousand pounds. She felt an overpowering urge to open them and see what words could be so dangerous and had to take a firm hold on her morals to put them in her reticule unread.

"I'll take you home," Ronald said. "And for God's sake, Di, stay there. I have an ocean of work I should be doing at the office. Harrup has entrusted some very weighty matters to me. He says that if I can handle the responsibility and prove valuable to him, he'll see I get some sinecures that will more than double my salary. In case I want to get married in the future, you know." His disillusioned eye spoke loud of the unlikelihood of such a circumstance.

"That is kind of him," Diana said. "I hope you have some money, Ronald. I've used up all Harrup gave me. It seemed such a lot, too."

"I can afford to hire a cab, at least."

They soon hailed a passing cab, and Diana suggested that Ronald's time was more valuable than hers, so she would go home last. In fact, she wasn't eager to go home at all. It was true she had recovered the letters, but as she surveyed the morning, she saw some unpleasantness in telling Harrup the details. Over two hundred pounds spent, to say nothing of the wrecked curricle. Worst of all was the damage done to his gray's mouths. She doubted that would please him.

Her own shoulder ached quite badly, but all these details couldn't explain her gloomy mood. She had a fine rout to look forward to that evening—that should cheer her. Any thought of that do only cast her into deeper misery. It would be Harrup's first formal appearance as Selena's fiancé. That set the seal on their approaching marriage, somehow. Why should that bother her? Hadn't she done everything in her power to make the marriage possible? Of course she had, and she shouldn't have done it.

They were wretchedly mismatched. With the best of intentions, Harrup would not long be satisfied with that simpering miss for a wife. He'd be back to his women, falling into more scrapes, and she wouldn't be there to participate. She'd be back at the dull Willows, hearing from Peabody what new activities Harrup was engaged in. Lady Selena would be unhappy; Ronald would be heart-broken. It was kind of Harrup to have given Ronald such an important job—and the hope of some sinecures to increase his salary, too. Before too long, Ronald might be able to set up a small house, which would require a hostess. . . . She would

159

be seeing Harrup more frequently than in the past if that happened.

And he would be married to Selena—much good seeing him would do her! Was that what caused her dismal thoughts? The notion that once the marriage took place, he would be forever off limits to her? She was no lightskirt, to enjoy an affair with him. She was nothing—just a country neighbor who had intruded herself into his exciting life for a few days. She wished she and Peabody had never delivered his billets-doux from Whitby. She wished she had never come to know him intimately. He was a libertine and a scoundrel—and she loved him so much her heart ached to think of his marrying Selena.

Chapter Eleven

Diana arrived home none the worse in appearance, despite her tribulations. Peabody was so busy harassing the servants that she didn't even inquire where her charge had been. Diana planned to leave early the next morning for home. The rout would be her last meeting with Harrup. For one more night she must gird her loins and behave as normally as possible. It was unthinkable that he should guess her feelings. How had she come to love him? He was eminently unsuitable. Much too high in society and much too low in morals. His temper was unstable. A woman wouldn't have a moment's peace with such a man— nor a moment's boredom.

His wife would be active in the nation's affairs, not stuck in a provincial backwater, doing the same tedious nothings forever. She could speak her mind quite freely with him, for whatever his faults, Harrup didn't mind plain speaking. She smiled ruefully to think what the vicar back home would say if he heard of her doings that day. Harrup might be angry about his horses, but for the rest, he wouldn't care a groat that she'd been arrested. He was fortunate he wasn't under lock and key himself after knocking the Prince Regent's brother senseless. She rather looked forward to telling him her adventures.

As the afternoon wore on, the preparations for the party

were finished, and Diana went upstairs to begin her toilette. She was dismayed to see the bruise on her shoulder was turning to purple, making her only evening gown impossible to wear. The gown was cut low, revealing the discoloration. Was she not to have this last evening with Harrup after all? A tear scalded her eye. She would attend the party if she had to wear the lutestring that sat in a mess in her suitcase. Peabody had thought a couple of good cushion covers might be made from the skirt.

She went through her belongings and settled on a paisley scarf to wear over her shoulders. Its somber hue added nothing to her ensemble, but at least it hid the bruise. She dressed her hair, brushing it till it shone in the lamplight. Her pixie eyes didn't give their usual impression of high spirits as she gazed at them. They were shadowed with sorrow that was emphasized by the downward turn of her lips. She forced a smile that looked grotesque. She was very pale, too.

While she was rubbing her cheeks to simulate the work of Mrs. Whitby's paint, a discreet knock came at the door. "Come in, Peabody," she called.

A servant ducked her head in and said, "His lordship's home and would like to see you downstairs if you're decent, Miss Beecham."

A jolt of excitement did more to color Diana's cheeks than the rubbing. Her eyes lit up like magic, and she said breathlessly, "Thank you, Marie. I shall be down directly."

She checked to see that the shawl was doing its work, then ran to the staircase. She had an intuition that Harrup would be there at the bottom, waiting for her. She had envisaged a glowing eye, an outstretched hand, and was disappointed to see only the spread of uninterrupted marble floor. When she reached the hall, his office door was open, the lamps lit, and she went toward that room.

Harrup was leaning over his desk, rifling through the

162

clutter of papers. He turned at the sound of her entrance and looked up. She saw no secret love glowing there, no warm smile of welcome, but only a raised brow and a questioning look.

Then he smiled softly, and all those imaginary items fell into place, exactly as she had imagined. There was a spontaneous warmth, a disarmingly real pleasure on his face as he looked at her. "I see you made it home intact. Tell me all about it," he invited, drawing up a chair.

"Have you spoken to Ronald?" she asked, suddenly nervous now that the waited-for moment had arrived.

Harrup poured two glasses of wine and handed her one. "Not since I sent him off with my bits of blood this morning. Did he find you? And, more important, did you have any luck with the letters?"

"Yes, I recovered them," she said.

He stared in disbelief. "You didn't!" he exclaimed. "I made sure it was a lost cause."

Encouraged that she had succeeded beyond his expectations, her other fears subsided. "Indeed I did. If you will ring for Stoker, I'll send him for them. They're in my reticule this moment."

Harrup drew a chair beside hers and said, "Later. Tell me all about it. Right from the moment I left you. I haven't been able to concentrate all day, wondering what you were up to. They must be thinking they've made a demmed poor choice in the cabinet. I was babbling like an idiot at the meeting."

Diana took a sip of wine while she arranged her story. "Well," she said hesitantly, "before I say anything else, Harrup, I want to assure you your team is safe and sound— nearly."

His eyes flew to her face. "How nearly?" he asked.

"Practically perfect. Just perhaps a little cut at the mouths, for they are more difficult to control than I had

163

thought. The traffic is very heavy on Bond Street, is it not?''

"Very heavy. A little cut will soon heal," he said generously. "So what happened? How did you get the letters?''

"They were in a safe-deposit box, as she said. The New Bank of England, actually. It was Ronald who spotted her going in."

"Did she not see you following her? I'm surprised she'd get them out when she was being watched."

"She didn't recognize me. I bought a new bonnet and pelisse."

"You must show them to me later."

"That won't be possible, I fear. I gave them to a . . . a young woman who—who needed them," she said vaguely.

Harrup frowned but didn't lose track of the main thread. "How did you get Whitby to give up the letters?" he demanded.

"She didn't exactly give them up, Harrup. I stole them from her when she was unconscious."

"Diana, you didn't hit her on the head in the middle of Bond Street?"

"Oh, no, I didn't hit her at all. And it happened on Glasshouse Street, when she was nearly home. I couldn't let her go into the house with the letters, Harrup. We might never have found them," she told him with such a pleading look in her eyes that Harrup turned quite pale.

"What happened on Glasshouse Street?" he asked in a voice that he was trying very hard to keep calm.

"Your team . . . got away from me a little."

"They didn't get into Mrs. Whitby's carriage and take the letters from her bosom. What did you do?"

"Don't look so horrid, Harrup!" she exclaimed. "They didn't lay any charges against me at Bow Street, and besides, I didn't use my own name."

164

"Oh, God!" Harrup raised one hand to his forehead and covered his eyes. "You were arrested."

"I didn't mention your name at all! How can you think me such a flat? After they searched me and didn't find the papers, they let me off with a warning."

"Searched you?" he asked, eyes flashing. "*Searched you?* Diana, why, in the name of God, didn't you call me? They actually stripped you—I never meant for you to go to such lengths to get the damned letters. She only wanted money for them. I would gladly have paid. By God, I'll have Whitby whipped at the cart's tail for this piece of impertinence."

"It's all over and done with. They didn't find anything except your money. I still had most of it then. I convinced the woman who examined me that I had got it from a customer."

His glowering eyes turned a shade darker with wrath, yet with some bright glitter of curiosity that made them so luminous they looked ready to explode. "That was before I had to pay the damages to Mrs. Whitby's rig," she explained. "They said if we paid, we wouldn't be charged, since it was an accident, you know. I didn't run the curricle into her carriage on purpose."

"But you *did* run my new curricle into her carriage?" he asked in a voice of silken menace.

"One wheel—"

His frown softened. "A wheel can be replaced," he said leniently.

"One wheel won't have to be replaced," she admitted. "The rest of it, I fear, is totally destroyed. I got the letters though," she reminded him brightly.

"You still haven't told me how!"

"It was the greatest luck, Harrup. I regained the use of my wits before Mrs. Whitby," Diana told him, peering uncertainly from the corner of her eye.

His face went blank. For full thirty seconds he was com-

165

pletely speechless. "You're telling me you were knocked senseless, along with all the rest! Yes, I know," he added, holding up a peremptory hand to silence her. "You got the letters. The devil take the letters! I didn't want you to start a riot to recover them and maim yourself into the bargain."

"Rubbish," she said, dismissing Bow Street, accidents, and other varieties of mayhem with the word. "No one was maimed, I promise you. Mrs. Whitby wasn't even limping, though she was very pale beneath her rouge. Did you know she painted, Harrup?" she asked with an arch smile.

Harrup shook his head and grinned. "Cat! I'm surprised you found time to notice that. Are you truly all right, Diana?"

She looked down at herself. "As you see, right as rain. And now will you please send Stoker for the letters. I am dying to read them."

Harrup's jerked to attention. "Read them? That wasn't part of our bargain!" He rang for Stoker and sent him after Diana's reticule.

Harrup regarded his companion and shook his head. "I told myself a dozen times this day that I was imagining problems where none existed. I thought the most you would do was embarrass yourself and possibly job my horses. It's well I was left in ignorance of the facts. What possessed you to go so far out of your way for me?"

The question took her by surprise. Why had she? It was really none of her affair if Harrup was embarrassed. He could well afford to buy Whitby's silence for that matter, so why had she pitched herself into such an imbroglio? The truth ambushed her, making her ill at ease. A flush started at her collarbone and rose up her throat, staining her cheeks. She had done it because it was her instinct to defend and protect the man she loved, and the guilty truth glowed in her eyes. Harrup gazed at her with a matching look. It was easy to imagine he shared her feelings and her frustration

166

at having to remain silent. Certainly some emotion raged in him, and a trace of it escaped into his eyes. A long silence grew between them, a conscious, uncomfortable silence.

Harrup cleared his throat nervously and tried to talk the feeling away. "Well, in any case I thank you most humbly, Diana," he said heartily. Too heartily. The lack of ease in this usually polished gentleman was quite noticeable. "Such an outstanding act of heroism deserves a reward. Name it, and it's yours."

She searched desperately for something to lighten the mood and said inanely, "I couldn't let Ronald's patron fall into disgrace. If you lose your position, Ronald loses his as well."

Harrup's look, the half smile at the corner of his lips, told her without words how much credence he placed in this explanation. The feeling was back in the air between them, a suffocating blanket of swirling emotion that eddied to and fro with each quick flicker of the eyes, each jerky movement of the hand, each thud of the heart, and each rapid breath. It would take more than a piece of idle chatter to dissipate it. Diana felt that if Harrup didn't say something, she would throw herself into his arms and tell him she loved him. She read the uncertainty in his gaze, the hopeful question, but she read the dread that was there, too. It was best to leave it unspoken.

Diana was relieved when Stoker came with her reticule. It made a diversion to her discomfort. Harrup went to the door and handed her the bag. She opened it and drew out the two infamous letters. Harrup reached eagerly for them. He pulled out the sheets and glanced at them, then quickly stuffed them back into their envelopes.

"They're the originals," he said, and took a quick step toward the grate, where a fire burned desultorily.

Diana jumped up from her seat and ran after him. "You can't burn them! I haven't read them yet!" she said.

167

"That is precisely why I am in a hurry to consign them to the flames."

"You said I have earned a reward. I have only to name my price. I want to read the letters," she insisted. "Just a quick glance. I have been dying to know what nonsense is in them."

Harrup held them to the flames, one in either hand. "You would only be further disillusioned with me," he said. "You already have me pegged for a libertine and a wastrel. Must you know to what depths of folly a man in his cups can sink? Leave me a shred of self-respect," he said, and watched with satisfaction as the papers caught fire. When only an inch of white paper remained, he dropped them into the grate and turned back to her. "I am already black enough in your judgmental eyes."

"You'll soon be rid of my judgmental eyes. Peabody and I will be leaving tomorrow morning," she said, and looked hopefully for some sign of objection.

Harrup frowned, but made no demur. "Yes, I thought you would. I shall miss you, Diana. It was pleasant having you—a woman—someone here to come home to," he ended uncertainly. "A strong-willed shrew to beat and lecture and joke me into rectitude. I know what you're going to say," he continued swiftly. "Soon Lady Selena will be here, but my sentiments in that respect are no secret to you. I half feel I'm adopting a daughter and losing my wife. Timing is so important, Laura said this morning. She was right about that. Our timing was very bad, was it not, my dear?" he asked gently.

It was as much as he could say, and though even that might more properly have remained unsaid, she was glad he had bent the rules of propriety. It was important to know that you were loved, and it was love that glowed in his eyes, love that strained the muscles of his face till he looked rigid, like the stone martyrs on the tombs in church. She felt tears spring to her eyes and blinked them away. "Thank you, Harrup. That will be my reward," she answered in an unsteady voice, just before she turned to flee the room.

"This is not a reward. It's a sentence," he said gruffly.

Diana went to her room and flung herself on the bed to cry. Harrup soon went upstairs to change. As he shaved, his brow was furrowed with schemes. When he stood at the mirror arranging his cravat, an expression of unholy conniving settled on his saturnine features. Dare he ask a favor of Laura Whitby after such harsh treatment as she'd received at his hands? It was outrageous—but it would surely turn Groden against him. Markwell was in a very insecure position at Whitehall with himself now the attorney general. If he wished to make any strides in his career at all, he'd be eager to ingratiate his superior. And Markwell must have some influence with Mrs. Whitby. The irony of what he contemplated after Di's efforts on his behalf was by no means lost on him. She'd scratch his eyes out—just before her pixie smile beamed and he kissed her.

He hurried to his desk and wrote up two letters of purpose prose, addressed them to Mrs. Whitby, and locked them in his desk. Next he wrote a brief note to Markwell. Markwell had been on the fidgets about not receiving an invitation to this evening's do. He'd jump at the offer to come around after dinner.

This done, Harrup stuck a diamond stud in his shirt front and went downstairs to welcome his guests, every one of whom he was eager to see leave.

Chapter Twelve

A smaller number of guests were invited to Harrup's dinner than to the rout afterward. The Grodens were there, the Eldons, and Lord Liverpool, along with the foreign minister and Harrup's house guest, Diana. Ronald was induced to attend, but Peabody announced firmly she had no business hobnobbing with smarts and swells and would take her mutton with Mrs. Dunaway and Stoker early, to be on the alert during the guests' dinner. "For you may rest assured everything will go wrong," she forecast glumly.

Nothing went very far wrong. It is true Ronald knocked over his wineglass, but it was nearly empty—nothing a well-placed serviette couldn't hide. Lady Selena sulked all through the fish and only smiled when she caught Ronald's eye, which occurred more often than was seemly. She called Lord Castlereagh Lord Eldon more than once and appeared to think Eldon was the prime minister. But then, no one paid much attention to her, for by and large, she was silent as a jug.

Diana was also quiet. She did, at least, take a keen interest in the conversation around the table, however, and had no trouble conversing with her immediate partners. The handsome Lord Castlereagh was very adept at flirting with pretty ladies who admired him. He kept up a lively patter of anecdotes about the Congress of Vienna that nearly made her forget for a few moments this was her last evening with Harrup.

The host, Diana observed, was distracted. He made a token of talking to his partners, moved his food around on his plate, and sipped his wine, but his fork seldom rose to his lips. Once she noticed him staring at her, not her face, but her shoulder. She glanced down and saw her shawl had slipped, revealing the bruise. She lifted the shawl to cover it and peeked again at Harrup. His brows rose in a silent question. She hunched her shoulders and smiled. Harrup shook his head and lifted his eyes ceilingward.

When dinner was finished, the ladies left the gentlemen to their port and removed to the saloon. Lady Selena received her fair share of attention then, for the quizzes were all eager to spot a flaw in the sullen beauty.

"So you have attached Lord Harrup. That is quite a coup, my girl," Lady Castlereagh informed her.

Selena looked on with serene indifference. "My papa arranged it."

"When is the wedding to be?" Lady Castlereagh asked.

"Whenever they tell me. I have nothing to say about it," Lady Selena answered, then rose and changed her seat. She chose to sit beside Ronald's sister. "How did your brother do at his new job, Miss Beecham?" she asked.

"Very well, I believe," Diana answered, and turned aside to inform Lady Castlereagh that her brother was Harrup's assistant, hoping to imply this was Selena's only interest in him.

Lady Castlereagh answered in a low voice. "If you want my opinion, Miss Beecham, Harrup is making a dreadful mistake. That young chit is not at all up to snuff. I'm surprised Groden hasn't taken her in hand. You may rest assured Harrup will soon do it. He will not put up with her sighing and sulking ways. Furthermore, she is too young for him—though monstrously pretty, of course."

It was an uncomfortable half hour during which Selena

only spoke voluntarily to Diana, while snubbing the wives of the most important government leaders. To Diana, she spoke only of Ronald. It was with a sigh of relief that Diana heard the approach of the gentlemen. Harrup came toward his future bride and tried to engage her in harmless banter till it was time for the other guests to arrive. The bride-to-be paid him only scanty attention. Her interest obviously lay across the room, where Ronald was caught up in conversation with Lord Eldon.

At nine o'clock the other guests began arriving for the rout. Diana went immediately to the ballroom to see that all was in order there. She was staggered to see one of the first arrivals was Lord Markwell. In a tizzy of disbelief she went searching for Harrup, who was greeting guests at the doorway.

During a lull in arrivals she tugged his arm. "Harrup, Markwell is here!" she said.

"Yes, I have already made him welcome." He smiled blandly.

"You mean you invited him after what he tried to do to you?"

"Of course. He is a excellent employee in my department. Personal animosities cannot be carried over into work."

"A rout isn't work. I made sure you would snub him outside of the office."

"This function is work related. You don't think I voluntarily cavort with the likes of Eldon and Liverpool?" he asked, shocked. "This is my card of thanks for their kindness in my appointment. As it turns out, Markwell has this very evening performed an invaluable service for me."

Diana just shook her head. "I thought I had begun to understand you, but you've surprised me again."

"This has surprised you?" he asked, and laughed. "Wait till you discover the favor Markwell has done."

"If you tell me Mrs. Whitby is coming to your party as

well, I shall assume there is no limit and elope with Lord Castlereagh.''

"You've chosen your quarry ill. He won't be easy to detach from his lady. He's peculiarly fond of Amelia," he warned her. "A fine example to those like myself, who are about to embark on a matrimonial journey."

Diana stiffened perceptibly when this subject arose. She turned to leave, and Harrup touched her arm. "Save me a waltz. I'll be joining the dancers shortly," he said. That was all, but the searching smile that accompanied his short speech left her emotions in tatters.

The gentlemen, she decided, handled these tricky situations much better than she. Lord Markwell, who certainly knew who she was, made a point of being presented to her and stood up with her twice. He was an excellent dancer and amusing as well. When he had the impudence to express his joy on Harrup's promotion, he went too far.

"I expect Mrs. Whitby was also thrilled that I got away with her letters," she said frankly, hoping to jostle him out of his sangfroid.

Markwell emitted an uneasy little laugh. "It's the chance of the game," he said. "You win some, you lose some. At this point, I expect madam is nearly as confused as I am myself."

"She is not as confused as I," Diana declared, and decided to forget the whole affair.

Half her attention was on the doorway, where she expected to see Harrup appear at any moment. When he finally came, he was with the entire Groden family, and his first dance was with Selena. She noticed that he didn't bother trying to prod the girl into conversation. While Selena looked around the room for Ronald, Harrup was busy looking for someone, who Diana soon realized was herself. When he spotted her dancing with Lord Castlereagh, he smiled and stopped looking.

Diana wondered if he would have to stand up with Lady

Groden, too, before he could come to her. Perhaps Lady Eldon must be honored as well. She kept an eye on all these people while still enjoying her dance with Castlereagh. She saw Lord Groden called from the room by Stoker, and wondered what it could mean. In less than a minute Stoker was back, beckoning Harrup away. A sense of excitement was in the air. Markwell kept looking at her in a curious way. Soon Castlereagh began to wonder if something was amiss at Whitehall.

"It can't be," he decided. "Lord Liverpool is still overflowing one of the side chairs. If I see him being hauled to his feet, you must excuse me, Miss Beecham."

At the end of the dance Diana went to join her brother, to prevent him from running to Selena. While she went through the paces of a country dance with Ronald, Lord Harrup was summoned to his own office by an extremely irate Lord Groden.

He lowered his bushy eyebrows and shook two letters under Harrup's nose. "I have just been handed these missives, Harrup, and must demand an explanation of them."

Harrup took the two familiar sheets and conned them quickly. "They appear self-explanatory to me, milord," he answered blandly. "May I know where you got hold of them?"

"This Whitby woman," he said, jabbing at the letters, "had the effrontery to send her footman to this house to give them to me."

"What an extraordinary thing for Mrs. Whitby to do," Harrup answered. "Are you quite sure they weren't intended for me?"

"They were addressed to me, in this large envelope with a note. Mrs. Whitby says that I might be interested to learn the character of my future son-in-law. The character of that hussy is what I have learned. Forging notes . . ." He looked hopefully to Harrup, who stared at him in astonishment. "I know how these women behave. You have only

174

to give me your word these were not written by you, Harrup, and the matter is forgotten. The handwriting is not at all like yours, now I take a closer look at it.''

Harrup examined the letters more closely. "No, these are a couple of letters I wrote to Mrs. Whitby, actually."

"Now don't be rash, Harrup. Look again," Groden advised.

Harrup looked again. "They are definitely my letters," he insisted. "You will notice the date on this one is today. I would hardly forget so soon."

"But see here, you say 'when we were together last night.' You were at the party at Brooke's last night."

Harrup ground his teeth in frustration at this error. "Quite right. I ought to have said 'this morning,' It was certainly well past midnight when I visited Mrs. Whitby."

When Groden realized he had been outmaneuvered and must do the proper thing, he went into a fine bluster. "You can hardly expect me to hand over my innocent young daughter to a man who hasn't even the decency to deny he wrote these!" he pointed out.

"Would a lie enhance my eligibility?"

"No, sir, but behaving like a gentleman would. I must inform you my wife will be sending in a retraction of the engagement to the papers this very night."

"I am very sorry to hear it, sir," Harrup replied mildly.

"Hmpf! *Now* you will lie," Groden roared, and squashed the two letters in his fist.

Harrup stood like a rock, willing down the triumphant shout that he longed to break forth. He waited to see if Groden had any further abuse to heap on him, and when the old man only stood shaking his head, he spoke. "It was a bad idea from the start. I had no idea Selena was so, er, young," he said.

"I told you she was not quite eighteen."

"Eighteen or nineteen, you said."

"What odds? She is out, and she is fully developed, so

far as physique goes. A dandy-looking gel. Not a bright child, of course. I can see why you are reluctant to have her. Perhaps it is as well. My wife was not fully in favor of the match."

"The season is just beginning, Groden," Harrup pointed out. "An incomparable like Selena will be snapped up before you can say one, two, three. She will be very happy to hear the wedding is off."

"I won't pretend she hasn't been pouting and mooning about the house till I can hardly look at her without feeling like Jack Ketch. It would have been an entirely eligible match, though. An excellent match for her. The attorney general's lady, and that is just the beginning, if I know anything."

"I am honored at your confidence."

Groden cast a regretful glance at his host. "You'll go far, my lad. There are more twists in you than we knew. Thank God you're not a Whig."

"True blue and Tory, too. Shall we drink a toast to the party?" Harrup asked. The battle was won, but to ensure he hadn't lost a friend into the bargain, Harrup called for a bottle of his best champagne, and they drank their toast, chatting of this and that. "I hear Princess Charlotte is *enceinte*. That will be good for the mood of the country. Let us hope she gives Prinney a grandson," Harrup mentioned.

"That would be some compensation for his wretched marriage. My eldest is expecting as well, did you hear? It will be her third. A good, fertile lass, and she gives us sons, too."

"That makes ten grandchildren in all now, I believe?"

After one glass, the two gentlemen returned to the party. There was no scandalous storming out of Harrup's house, wife and daughters in tow, but the Grodens did depart early. Lady Groden was informed by her spouse that she had a migraine and wished to leave. Lady Selena couldn't be counted on to conceal her joy at the news and didn't learn she had escaped Harrup's clutches till she had reached home. She was so happy she cried for ten minutes before she fell sound asleep.

Diana watched from the sidelines when Groden and Harrup returned from the study. She observed there was no breach between them—in fact, Harrup was smiling and Groden looked no more fierce than usual. She saw the family take a polite leave, and while they left early, the evening was by no means just beginning. A few of the other elderly guests were beginning to pull out their watches and stroll purposefully toward the door as well.

Still following Harrup with her eyes, Diana watched him go to the orchestra and speak to the head fiddler. From there he came directly to her. It was impossible to interpret the gleam in his eyes, the smile he couldn't quite hold in check, and impossible for her not to assume the same tokens of joy.

"Time for our waltz," he said. As the beguiling strains of Weber's music filled the room, he drew Diana into his arms to whirl around the floor till her head spun. A dozen questions were begging for answers, but there would be time for that later. Now she wanted to enjoy the too brief pleasure of being in his arms, swirling and spinning in dizzying circles, forgetful of tomorrow and all the dull tomorrows after.

Harrup, his mind seething with thoughts of his own, appeared satisfied with her silence. It wasn't till the dance was over and he led her to a seat that he noticed they hadn't exchanged a word. "Chatterbox. Setting up in competition with Selena, are you, Di?" he asked. "That was my second wordless dance this evening."

"I had a dozen things I wanted to ask you, but the music was too wonderful to spoil. Oh, dear, and now you must go. I see the Eldons are edging toward the door. Your friends aren't very lively partygoers, are they?"

"My friends are; my colleagues are less frivolous. Tomorrow is another working day. We'll talk as soon as I get the last of them blasted off.''

In an effort to hasten this moment along, a midnight dinner was served at eleven-thirty. The younger guests who hoped for another round of dancing after dinner were disappointed. The orchestra had been dismissed while they ate. With these little hints staring them in the face, they soon took their leave. Strangely, Lord Markwell was the last to leave.

"Did everything work out all right, Harrup?'' he asked as he was being handed his coat by Stoker.

"Excellently. You must thank our mutual friend for me.''

"You won't forget to put in a word for me when they are choosing new privy councillors?'' he mentioned. His speech indicated this subject had arisen before. Diana was bewildered at the man's gall and Harrup's calm acceptance of it.

"You have my vote,'' Harrup assured him.

Polite good-nights were exchanged; the door was closed on the last guest and bolted with a sigh of relief by Stoker. "A nice early party, your lordship,'' he said.

"Nicer than you know, Stoker.'' Harrup smiled, and putting his arm familiarly around Diana's shoulder, he drew her toward his office. This breach of good taste surprised her. With a blighting look she lifted the offending arm and entered the room by herself.

"I feel I am one of your colleagues,'' she said. "We always seem to talk in your office.''

"The servants will be breaking glasses and spilling drinks in the saloon,'' he explained. "We will be more private here.''

She turned a questioning face toward him. "Do you have something to say that requires privacy?'' The diabolical light in his eyes told her he had and set her pulse pounding with hope. "Harrup, what has been going on here tonight?

Why did you let that weasel of a Markwell come, and treat him with special respect, too?''

"I'm sure I explained that already."

"You didn't explain why you would support his bid for privy councillor."

"That was for services rendered."

She thought for a moment and could make no sense of it. "I know you're up to something. How dare you leave me out of it? What favor has he done for you?" she demanded.

"He had coerced Mrs. Whitby into helping me," he admitted.

"Helping you what? I am the one who got you out of that muddle. Harrup—she didn't have more letters!"

"She did, actually," he said, and smiled softly.

"You're hopeless. I don't know when you ever found time to be a privy councillor. Between romancing Mrs. Whitby in person and writing your maundering drivel to be blackmailed with, you mustn't have had much time to spare for work. You said there were eight letters. I recovered eight. What new ones are these?"

"These are the two I wrote her this evening," he said.

Diana felt like a bull taunted by a red flag. "You couldn't stay away from that painted hussy, could you?" She blinked and stared at him as though he were Satan incarnate. Bereft of words to express her outrage, she turned on her heel and marched to the door. Harrup got there a minute before her and blocked her exit. Taking her by the arm, he led her back and gently pushed her into a chair. When she spotted a bottle of champagne and two glasses on his desk, with a small purple velvet box on the tray beside the glasses, she didn't bolt up from the chair. Harrup opened the wine and poured two glasses, handed her one.

She lifted her chin and tossed her head, ignoring it. Harrup raised her hand and placed her fingers around the stem. "To us, Di," he said softly. His smile was enigmatic.

"Which 'us' is that, Harrup? You and me and Lady Selena? Or is it you and me and Mrs. Whitby? Perhaps all four of us? I have heard of romantic triangles, but if you actually think to involve me in a—a *rectangle*, I must tell you—"

"I have no interest in polygons. A straight line is what I shall be walking in future. A straight line, the shortest distance between two points, if memory serves."

Her heart began thudding in her chest. Two rose circles, very similar in appearance to Mrs. Whitby's rouge, blushed on her cheeks. Harrup was unaware of them. He was gazing into her blue pixie eyes, where that hardy, intangible hope gleamed once more. Her breaths came in rapid, light gasps. "You wouldn't recognize a straight line if you fell over one," she said unevenly.

His lips quivered in delight. "What use would a couple of renegades like us have for straight lines? To us," he repeated, and lifted his glass to touch hers. The delicate tinkle of crystal on crystal was the only sound in the room. A pall of silence sat around them. Diana slowly lifted her glass, looking at him over its rim, and sipped the champagne.

"And now will you tell me what happened?" she asked, setting the glass aside.

"Soon. First I mean to eliminate the distance between us." Harrup put his glass aside and drew Diana up from her seat into his arms. She was crushed to his chest while his lips pressed ruthlessly on hers. She felt again the heady sensation of the waltz, as though she were adrift on a sea of sensation, cut loose from dreary reality. She spun in a world where any wonderful thing was possible. Where Harrup was hers, incredibly, in love with her, and a mere bride and mistress were irrelevant.

She had never been kissed so thoroughly or so long before. Nothing had prepared her for the sweep of emotions that surged over her, making her want to cry and laugh, to dance and shout and sing all at once. His lips moved hungrily on hers, and she answered every demand, with her arms curling around his neck to hold him to her.

When he eventually lifted his head, she saw his wild gaze, the pupils dilated till his eyes looked black. There was no mischievous smile now, but a sober gentleness that was new. She had no idea what he would say.

"Diana, you know me with all my faults," he said simply. His voice was low, ragged, and uncertain. "I'm not a very worthy man. My past is littered with indiscretions, but with you to manage me, I can be as good as you care to make me. I never cared enough before to want to please anyone but myself," he continued, his tone becoming firmer as he saw the acceptance in her eyes. "I find myself, now, wondering what Di would think of my actions. You have shown me how a gentleman ought to behave, and that such behavior need not be piously sanctimonious—in fact, it can be more fun than lechery. But I doubt I can keep up your standards without you here to remind me from time to time. Will you marry me?"

Her heart soared into the ether. "I will, Charles." She sighed. "But—"

His lips silenced her, and for a long moment they clung together.

"But are you sure you won't tire of me, as you tired of Selena and Mrs. Whitby? I daresay the charms of a nag would wear thin very soon, she warned.

"The nagging will cut two ways, my dear. We shall see who cries craven first. My first nagging has to do with—this," he said, pushing aside her shawl and touching the bruise on her shoulder. He gazed at it a moment, softly grazing it with warm fingers. "I was appalled when I saw it at dinner—and you didn't even tell me. There will be no more exploits from me that require you to do battle with Runners and lightskirts.''

"Make that just lightskirts, Charles, if you please. I enjoyed the rest, but *that* must come to an end. I have already told you I mean to marry for love. I—I *do* love you very much,'' she said shyly. "I mean, I wouldn't want you to think it's only the title and your money, though they're very nice, too, of course.''

His eyes crinkled in a smile. "As well as the handle and money, I solemnly undertake to provide your full conjugal quota of lonely nights and anxiety, but unless you find it in your heart to be jealous of members of Parliament, I must warn you there will be no cause for jealousy.''

She considered it a moment in playful silence. "Two out of three isn't bad. And now, will you please give me my ring. I have been trying to keep my eyes from wandering to the tray. And tell me whether I have to devise a scheme to be rid of Lady Selena, or have you already taken care of it?''

"I thought it more proper to handle the jilting myself,'' he said. He took the velvet box from the tray and opened it. A star sapphire gleamed in a nest of white satin.

She gasped with pleasure. "Oh, Charles! I thought it would be a diamond. They're so cold they look like a chip of ice. This is lovely.''

He slid it onto her finger. "A star sapphire, to match your eyes. I never did put it in writing, did I? I knew when I saw it at Rundell's and Bridge's that it was meant for you.''

She gave him a long, sideways look. "Did you originally buy it for Mrs. Whitby?''

"Diana!'' he exclaimed indignantly. "I'm not *that* bad—to be giving the woman I love a cast-off mistress's cast-off present! Good God, I was hours searching town for just the right stone. I left work early this afternoon and bought it. I knew when you made me follow Laura that you loved me as I loved you. Despite your tirade, you loved me. I just hadn't figured out yet how we could manage to overcome a few obstacles. I nearly gave it to you this afternoon when I came home. It was burning a hole in my pocket."

"Why didn't you?"

"I was engaged to Lady Selena at the time."

"Charles, how did you get out of it?"

"Sharpen your claws, madam wife, and prepare to scratch my eyes out." He took a deep breath and told his tale. When it was done, she crossed her arms and scowled.

"You wrote to her again after I went to so much trouble to steal her letters? Charles, how could you?"

"I got Markwell's promise she wouldn't take them to the newspapers. It was only Groden I wanted to see them. I needed some excuse to make him call off the match, for it was plain as a pikestaff he wouldn't let Selena do it, and a gentleman is not permitted to act wisely in these affairs. God, it was touch and go. He all but begged me to let on I hadn't written the letters, though he knew perfectly well I had. Of course he didn't know when or why. The hell of it is, he didn't really care that I was visiting my mistress within days of my betrothal. All that mattered was that he could pretend he didn't know. Once I forced him to acknowledge it, he did the proper thing and rescinded his acceptance of my offer for Selena."

"He didn't seem very angry when he left. I had no idea what had happened."

"Party solidarity. No rift in the ranks, or the demmed Whigs might slip into power."

"Selena must be in alt." Diana smiled. "I wonder if Ronald might—"

"Not till we can heap a few honors and some more money on him, I fear. That is why I made him my assistant and let him dally a little with Selena to keep that fire simmering. Groden would never accept a man without a handle to his name, unless he had a fortune. If the romance survives her reading of *Waverly*, something might come of it eventually. I know Ronald will have two able abettors in Lord and Lady Harrup," he added, squeezing her fingers.

"Lady Harrup," she mused, spreading her fingers and smiling fondly at her ring. "We cannot announce the engagement for a while, I suppose. It would look so very odd, coming right on top of your other engagement."

"Nine days is usually the time span for wonders to cease being wonders. I think a man in my position ought to allow a little longer," he said unhappily.

"We'll have a short engagement—just long enough for me to go home and arrange my trousseau. I little thought when Peabody received your letter at the Willows how our visit to London would end." She sighed happily. "I wonder if she will be happy or take the match in aversion."

"Chuggie will talk her around," he said, confident of his way with Peabody.

"Make the envelope nice and thick. You have no idea how your reputation soars after she receives one of your bribes. Oh, Charles! We must ask Peabody to come to us after—I mean when we need someone for the nursery! That will be even better than money."

"Much better than money," he agreed. Charles gazed into space, visions of a new and different future before him. A future with a growing family, a prospering career, and his enchanting, pixie-eyed wife to keep him from *too* much propriety.

By the year 2000, 2 out of 3 Americans could be illiterate.

It's true.

Today, 75 million adults...about one American in three, can't read adequately. And by the year 2000, U.S. News & World Report envisions an America with a literacy rate of only 30%.

Before that America comes to be, you can stop it...by joining the fight against illiteracy today.

Call the Coalition for Literacy at toll-free **1-800-228-8813** and volunteer.

**Volunteer
Against Illiteracy.
The only degree you need
is a degree of caring.**

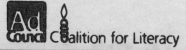

Ad Council   Coalition for Literacy

LV-2